Praise for

STARSEDGE: NEL BENTLY

TRAVELERS

"It would be no surprise if some people thought Nel, the heroine of *Travelers*, was a Lara Croft copy but she's not, and even admits that she's "no Lara Croft" when she finds herself in a situation that Ms Croft would have handled with only slight discomfort, if any at all. Nel is her very own character and solves her problems in her own unique way – no need to compare her to anyone, and I'm sure she'll become even more of a unique character in future adventures. I'm sure she'll have quite a few interesting challenges to deal with, probably also on the romantic side. I found her love interest a fairly intriguing character, and can see how her own heritage could cause some issues in future novels.

The writing style of the book made it easy to read and the author found a great balance here...I'd definitely recommend this book to people who enjoy the idea of aliens having been here before, and having left signs that can be found if people only dig deep enough (literally digging in this novel!)."

- Reader's Favorite

"*Travelers* by V. S. Holmes kicks off the Starsedge series, in which an acid-tongued archaeologist named Dr. Nel Bently makes her debut....Pinning a series on a single character is usually a risky move, but Holmes has certainly struck gold with Dr. Nel Bently. Nel is a bit like her beloved dig sites--the more time you spend with her, the more you'll uncover. Her outwardly gruff exterior is nicely balanced and buffered by a few key characters around her, and it's clear she cares about the undergrad students she works with, even if she sometimes struggles to be patient with them. The sci-fi elements are a bit underplayed in Travelers, but only because Nel is trying to puzzle out what exactly her team has stumbled upon. With answers--and, of course, more questions--served up later in the novel, the series can now take off in whichever direction it chooses."

- Red City Review

"I think I'm in love with this series. Grounded in the solid bedrock of real archeological techniques and experience, it takes off from there into the fantastic. I love it the way I love Tony Hillerman's writing: it challenges me to research new areas of study without once losing the draw of a gripping narrative. Even better, it shows truly rounded queer characters whose sexuality is just one facet of a complex and engaging personality. From page 1 Nel tromped through my imagination with a screw-you-too grin and a trowel in her back pocket. Her description of the field life feels incredibly real. This book rocks."

-O. E. Tearmann, author of *The Hands We're Given*

"The whole concept this story is based on and built around is fascinating, the way V.S. Holmes has written the characters and plot is brilliant... a suspenseful read with lots of surprises, a touch of romance, and a whole lot of promise..."

-Serena Yates of *Rainbow Book Reviews*

DRIFTERS

"Another clever and cocksure tale. Holmes pulls it off again with her absolutely driven Nel. Nothing, from hypothermia to the FBI, is going to stop this girl. Grit, friendship and deciding what to fight for when the future is bleak gives this a surprising emotional oomph to layer over the down-to-earth survival story. I read it straight through and wanted more."

-O. E. Tearmann, author of *The Hands We're Given*

STRANGERS

"You can tell V has an incredible grasp of who these characters are and we benefit from that right away. There are so many snappy bits of dialogue and interaction, there is what I call great over the shoulder moments that turn us around and look back at this or that, and there is this underlying tension that really is handled so well in the writing. It's nice when an author treats its audience like grown-ups. I also love that this story gives us just enough when we need it and so much just when we think we are about to settle in. It's easy to picture all this in your head, very cinematic, and a great puzzle as well."

-Joe Compton, author of *Amongst the Killing*

OTHER BOOKS BY
V. S. HOLMES

NEL BENTLY BOOKS
Travelers

Drifters

Strangers

Heretics

Fugitives

Emissaries

BLOOD OF TITANS WORLD
Smoke and Rain

Lightning and Flames

Madness and Gods

Blood and Mercy

SHORT FICTION
"Nowhere Fast" *(We Came to Dance)**

"Starfall" *(Vitality Magazine)*

"The Tempest" *(Out of the Darkness)*

"Disciples" *(Beamed Up)*

"Familiar Waters" *(Love and Bubbles)*

"Mere Primordium" (poem, *Mystic Blue Review*)

TRAVELERS

STARS EDGE: NEL BENTLY BOOK 1

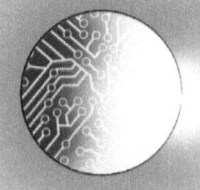

V. S. HOLMES

AMPHIBIAN PRESS

TRAVELERS

Copyright © 2016 by Sara Voorhis

Amphibian Press

P.O. Box 163

West Peterborough NH

03468

www.amphibianpressbooks.com
www.vsholmes.com
ISBN : 978-0-9961330-4-3

For those whose lives are built on shovels,
science, and sweat

AUTHOR'S NOTE

This series combines archaeology with science fiction. Doing so is a hazardous road, particularly with the advent of television like "Ancient Aliens" and the fourth Indiana Jones film.

This book is a work of fiction, and something to be enjoyed as entertainment. I wholeheartedly believe we are far from alone in the universe. That being said, I am an archaeologist by trade and I know humans are ingenious and resourceful enough to build pyramids and other architectural wonders all on their own.

ONE

Vandalism across a perfect site was the best recipe for an archaeologist's worst day. Apparently, it wasn't enough that Nel Bently's visa had met with "authenticity issues" twice on her way into Chile. She ducked under the rope that had served as a barrier. *A poor one*, she mentally snarled. The site was a disaster. Great gouges carved the formerly pristine soil. The tools stacked under a tarp by the bushes were now scattered, bent and broken. What pits her crew had dug the week before were filled with rotting leaves and back dirt, the perfect, square walls of the trenches ruined and crushed in.

Nel stepped carefully through the mess. *This has Founders written all over it.* As a rule, Nel was a patron of locals and the people she studied. Coming onto culturally significant land, not matter how old the site, was always tricky and she respected that. The Founders were her exception. They took issue with any archaeologist that set boots near their land, despite admitting there was no spiritual or cultural significance to the sites Nel chose.

"Well, fuck." Her tanned hand raked sweat and sunscreen through her sandy hair. She had permits and this was blatant vandalism. She turned back to her colleague and the two grad students who had arrived early to help. They waited, uncertain, at the rope, tools and packs still held with earnest dedication. "Alright, Mikey, grab pictures of this mess. You two, packs and tools go there, and set up a tent over them. Once Mikey has his pictures, clean it up. Wear gloves, it's gross and smells like a sewer."

She watched as they moved to do her bidding, eyes wide as they got their first good look at the vandalism. "If you need anything, talk to Mikey. I'll be on the phone." She trudged up the rise, dry soil crunching under her battered boots as she tugged the satellite phone from its case in her pack. She dialed, listening to the clicks as the call connected and surveying the land below her. It was perfect, really. The site was nestled between a stream and the rise she stood on now. The water had carved deep enough to have been there when it was inhabited, but small enough to be on only the local maps. The rise, curving from the north to the west, was covered with artifacts. It was the first place they surveyed, and it provided natural protection from the wind that whipped off the Pacific, just a few hundred feet away.

"You've reached the machine of Dr. Martin de Santos. Leave your name and number and how I can help you, and I'll return your call at the earliest convenience."

"Martos, it's Nel. Site was vandalized, looks like Founders. We could use some extra help—I don't know if my greens can handle this. Give my cell a call tonight, I'll be in town." As she hung up, she caught site of the rotted mess Mikey was about to shovel out. It was a rough shape of a symbol. "Oi! Mikey wait!" She snapped a few pictures with her handheld, before waving for him to continue and stamping down the rise. She had been unable to see it from the ground. It was the angled symbol with which the Founders signed their papers, websites and protests. As she watched the clean up, she noted two figures on the rise across the stream. Both wore telltale woven bands around their forearms. A cold mix of dread and defiance crawled down her spine. It wasn't like them to watch. *I'll be damned if I'm going to be cowed by radicals.* "C'mon," she called to the students, brown eyes fixed on the figures above. "I wanna see you moving dirt by ten!"

She returned to the site and sat on a rock, flipping through her field book. She had been digging since she was an undergrad. She had started with a history major, then steadily worked backwards in the time line, learning about anthropology, prehistorics, and paleolithics. She fell in love with her first dig. Now, with her doctorate defended, she had her own crew, her own research. Not to mention funding from a generous private patron to continue her passion for sweat, dirt, and work that made her body ache. She was staring at the page where she had sketched the site last summer when Mikey sauntered over.

He was a blocky man—square head, square hands, square shoulders—with only a slight paunch to round out the edges. "Sucks, eh? Think it was the Flounders?"

Nel smiled at his nickname for their adversaries. "More than likely. I tried to keep this site under wraps, but when you've grown up here, I think nothing escapes notice. They were watching us clean up this morning. Creeps me out a bit."

Mikey glanced at her, a frown crinkling his sun-weathered skin. Mikey was the resident prehistoric ceremonial specialist from their department, but more than that he was her best friend. "Everything okay?"

She shrugged. "I don't know." Her gaze was fixed on stain from rotted debris.

He rose with a groan. "I bet you a beer you pick up a shovel before tomorrow's over."

It was an old tradition. Nel could not keep her hands out the dirt, and even as site supervisor, she often found herself in a pit before long. She laughed. "You're on."

The Jeep ride back down to the village was about as comfortable as what Nel assumed a camel ride would feel like. The wheels bounced over a road that Class 6 trails in the U.S. dreamed of being when they grew up. It still made Nel feel decidedly badass. The trip took all of 30 minutes, though the distance was short, and it was close to 5:00 when they arrived. The house they rented for the summer—Vicuña y Las Rosas—was a small, narrow building, butted up against the hillside. A locked shed in the rear had enough room to park the Jeep and equipment, and that was all that mattered to Nel. She swung off the Wrangler's rollcage and began unloading.

"Go shower, get settled in if you didn't last night. Be downstairs in half an hour—I'm orienting the undergrads who arrived today. Dinner is whatever, wherever." When the students had scattered she felt Mikey's concerned gaze. She did not want that conversation. Not now.

"Meet you on the porch in twenty!" She hoisted her pack over her shoulder and grabbed the bag they used for the day's artifacts. She and Mikey had two of the singles on the fourth floor and with them the privilege of a private bathroom. The house was narrow and tall, giving the impression of precarious building. Nel knew it had survived every earthquake with minimal damage and had no qualms with her room at the very top. She dropped her field pack off in her room and spread out the finds on a desk in the spare room. Her fingers traced the artifacts. They were few, but promising.

Finally she grabbed her cooler and jogged down to the porch. Nel eased herself into a chair next to Mikey with a sigh. "What do you think this year'll bring?"

"Artifacts or crew?" Mikey popped open one of the precious ciders he shipped from the States.

"Crew. Artifacts are too close to home for me to comment on." The rest of the diggers arrived that afternoon. She wasn't looking forward to orientating a bunch of undergrads.

Mikey snorted, running fingers through his sweaty hair. "I think we'll get three partiers—old fashioned drunks—someone in a committed relationship and then the studious brown nose."

Nel laughed. "The usual round up?"

"Not every time. That one year everyone was a fucking introvert."

"You got a problem with that?"

"You kidding? That was the only year I got some decent sleep. Every other time it's either been drunkards stumbling up the stairs at 3:00 or someone boinking through the wall."

Nel raised her glass. "To introverts and celibates?"

Mikey hooted and tapped his bottle to hers. "Fuck yeah."

A door slammed above them and Nel smothered a smile. "I suppose I'll quiet down. They'll think I'm the partier among them."

Mikey laughed softly. "No, but you get a few beers and you'll be prowling the bars for a tanned-up senorita."

"She only chatted me up once, and it was my birthday." She leaned back with a smile. "You think she's still there?"

The screen door snapped open behind them and Mikey craned his neck to peer over. "Ahh, the crew approaches."

Four undergrads filed onto the porch. Each performed a rendition of the Where-Should-I-Sit dance before settling on the bench along the edge. Nel watched them shuffle about. She noticed more than a few puzzled glances directed at her and Mikey's un-showered appearance. *They'll be embracing dirty-beers soon enough.* A moment later her two grad students arrived and flopped, dirty, into the chairs.

When they stilled, she leaned forward, her eyes bouncing from one digger to the next. "Welcome to Chile. I'm Dr. Nel Bently and this is Dr. Michael Servais. We're heading up this year's field school for USNE. I know you all have to get settled in, you're welcome to skip dinner tonight. We do crew dinners every Wednesday. We'll get to know each other a bit now and the grad students will join us at the restaurant—Padradito's—a bit later. I know all of you by name, but you'll have to help me put faces to those names. Let's go around and introduce ourselves." The introductions were quick and awkward, Nel ignoring most of the innocuous why-I'm-an-arch-major nonsense as she tried to pin faces to names. *I'll learn about them over the next weeks. No sense wasting time now.*

When they finished, she polished off her beer and flipped open the cooler. "The social rules—I'll go over the work rules tomorrow on site—are simple. I know you're all of age, and we'll be drinking here, but try to keep the shenanigans to a minimum. Drink, but don't drive or be an asshole. Flirt with the local boys and girls, but don't get pregnant or knock someone up. Don't wander off alone. I don't have the budget for a drug lord's ransom, but that won't stop them from trying." The well-worn warning slid off her tongue and she added a narrow-eyed glare to the words. "Stay up late skinny dipping and bar hopping, but be out here on time in the morning. If you drink too much, you deserve the hangover." She made sure to punctuate the last statement with a heavy swig of her new bottle. "Now if you'll excuse me, I'm going to have a shower-beer."

The door clapped shut, muffling the stuttering conversation. She breathed a sigh of relief. She hated dealing with new people. She took advantage of the deserted upstairs by stripping off her dirt-logged clothes in the hall and almost skipping naked into the wet-bath. Within five minutes the solar-heated water ran red from the dirt ground into her skin.

Images of her vandalized site flashed through her mind. She slammed a fist against the tile. "Fuckers!" Her words echoed in the small room and she winced. There was no way Mikey didn't hear. The water was hotter than the day had been, and worked a few superficial knots from her back. *Man, there's nothing like a Phase II to screw up my back.* She stopped, soap forgotten in her hand. She had her own Phase II dig. Her excavation was fully funded by a third party and accredited through two universities. If under-grad-Nel saw her now she would never believe it. Nel tilted her head into the water with a happy sigh. Her mouth curled, eyes crinkling as they closed. *Someone pinch me, I'm dreaming.*

TWO

Nel crossed her arms and eyed the new students. "Welcome to Los Cerros Esperando VII. This is the seventh place we surveyed, thus the number. We're not looking for anything fancy here—nothing like Inca temples or crystal skulls. Aiming for projectile points, chipping debris, and manufacturing tools. If you don't know what a hammer stone looks like, come see me. Those of you who haven't worked with me, let me, Dr. Servais check your screen before you clear it. Just for the first week or so. The tools we're looking for are made of chert and scoria."

She pulled two artifact bags from her pocket and passed them around. "That point tip is chert, same with the flakes, just different varieties. The cone-thing is the leg to a molcajete made from scoria. Same material as those massive statues and heads you see. The layers we're finding the stuff in are consistent with 14-12 thousand years before present—though we haven't dated anything yet." The tools were weathered, but the scars from knapping were clean. The flakes were slightly curved, a tiny bulb where the force of the blow expanded out from the point of contact.

She scanned the crowd. They were silent, eyes large and fingers fiddling with new dig clothes. *They are so damned green.* "Alright. Safety briefing. Don't get hurt. Closest hospital is 53 minutes away - if you're hurt enough to need it, you'll probably die on the way there. If you find water, don't fall in it." She scanned down the generic site safety form. "No explosives here, no decon, no HazMat, no buried wires. If you're dizzy, sit, don't faint. Drink water. Eat food, but wash your hands and don't eat dirt or rocks."

She eyed Mikey taking a draw off his cigg. "If you're smoking, you shouldn't be and don't toss the butts. An artifact bag works nicely. If you have an epi-pen, please let us all know where you keep it. If you find an animal don't get bit or stung, but if you poke it, you deserve whatever happens." She glanced around at the faces, noting the mixture of startled entertainment and knowing smiles. *Nothing sets people at ease like joking about maiming and death.* "Any questions?"

One girl raised her hand. "Annie mentioned vandalism. What if that happens again?"

"I hope it won't. If it does we'll clean it up, document and so forth. The people we have to thank call themselves Los Pobladores—not the ones from Los Angeles, though. Do yourselves a favor and don't Google it. Usually those that do the vandalizing only do it the once." She jerked her head at the Jeep. "Most of the equipment we carry-in, carry-out, since that's the first that goes if we get vandalized. Questions?"

Annie raised a hand. "Are we opening Transect B now?"

"Some of you. I want to bust out A5, 7, and 11 before B starts." When no one spoke up, she clapped her hands. "Let's unload and get everyone acclimated. Mikey, get the seasoned diggers underway on the rest of Transect A."

She gathered the four greens by the Wrangler. They were all in their final year of undergrad, or had just graduated. Martos forbade her from accepting only grad students, but she drew the line at underclassmen. She would never have the necessary patience. "Alright, sorry for the repeat, but let's go around with names and backgrounds. I can remember most typologies, but can't handle names, it seems." She pointed at a girl with tan skin and a mass of blonde curls piled haphazardly into a bun.

"I'm Shiloh. I graduated from UNM where I studied Anthro. My minor was archaeology. This is my first non-school dig."

The next girl had a streak of sunblock through her thick eyebrow. "I'm Kat. I studied Archaeology at SUNY Platsburg and I'm going to BU to study lithics. I have an epi-pen in my pack, outer-most pouch, for bees. I dug in New England a bit with a few field schools."

George was a quiet Hispanic boy from New Orleans. An older girl named Sally leaned on the Jeep with the steady confidence of someone who knew her way around a site.

Nel unrolled the map across the Jeep's hood to show them the layout of the grid and where 50cm square test pits two years before had yielded stone tools and the flakes knapped off in the process of making them.

"We're standing to the north. Get yourselves oriented. Each black 'x' is a shovel test pit from two years ago. The black boxes are 1m square units we did last year. You'll see we alternated on the first line of a grid."

Finally she set them loose, pairing the newer students with those who were more experienced.

The day was long and hot. Nel was used to the thick pants that protected her legs from insects and metal, but she saw her students suffering. She ordered them to drink water every half hour, but most of them were unused to the work. Shiloh struggled with cleaning down the next 5cm level. Nel crouched at the edge of a pit they had cleaned out, tugging her trowel from the loop on her pants.

"Like this." She demonstrated. "See how the sharp edge works? Like scraping frosting off a cake." She watched the girl a few minutes more. "That's better. Don't use the handle, grip the butt of the blade. You'll get calluses before the week's out."

Her gaze flicked upwards at the sound of angry birds. A small flock rose from the hills bordering the site to the south. Her lips thinned and she rose. "Mikey, keep an eye out will you?" She jogged up the hill feeling the burn in her muscled thighs. The coastline arced away to her right, the line of hills and undulating scrubby grasslands falling away to her left. A small grove of twisted trees dotted the hilltop. Her eyes narrowed on the red, oozing wound carved across the closest tree. It was a single word, carved with a knife: *Hereje.* Her mouth twisted into a silent sneer. "You think carving 'heretic' on a fucking plant will scare me?" She spat the words into the shadows of the grove, but her heart lodged in her throat.

Nel needed to sort their finds from the day and file the paperwork, but anger still simmered and she would only make mistakes. *Better late than wrong.* She grabbed a six-pack from her paleo-aged mini-fridge and ducked out onto her fire escape.

Mikey was already perched on the dark roof, despite being the second to shower. He eyed the bottles in her hand. "Either you've suddenly become generous with your precious rehydration or you really need to vent."

She tried to shrug and sit at once and ended in an ungainly pile on the warm concrete beside him. She laughed, but her eyes were steely. "I'm fine. Just frustrated."

"'Fuckers'?" He quoted her mid-shower outburst from the day before.

"Heard that, did you?"

"Nel, this site is your baby. It's okay to feel shitty about this, or rebellious. Just don't get yourself in trouble. These people are locals. Their families cook our food and make our beds."

Nel wrinkled her nose. "Never heard a-one of the locals defending the Founders. They don't mess with them either."

"I dunno. We've been coming here forever, but I don't know if I could say I know them much better than when I was a green." He shrugged, tipping back his beer. "Today gave me the willies."

"They've never been violent before." Nel picked at the calluses at the base of her fingers. He had a point. A good one.

"They've never vandalized a site before. Not like this. Sure their symbol gets sprayed on our tents every summer and our shovels are usually sacrificed into the ocean, but this is weird."

"I know. Me too about the willies." Laughter swelled as the students exited the house and paraded down the road. The sound only distanced Nel more from the excitement.

"Did they watch today?"

Nel shrugged. "I didn't see them. They carved 'hereje' into a tree today." She heaved a sigh and drained her beer. "I was thinking about asking Maria about them." She named the owner of their house.

Mikey shot her a worried look. "They don't bug us and we don't bug them, Nel. Don't screw this up. If you're worried, call Martos."

"Fuck!" She shot to her feet. "I told him to call me last night!" She slid down the fire escape and through her window. Her phone blinked on the desk by the abandoned finds. She groaned and flipped it open. Martos' number glared up at her and she scrolled to his message.

"Nel, got your call. I was on the phone with our funders, actually. Sorry to hear about the site, as were they, but I don't think it's a big deal. The election down there probably has them all up in arms. I hope nothing was badly damaged. Shoot me an email when you can? Cheers."

She sighed and deleted the message before sinking onto her bed. Martos was great, but he had been out of the field long enough for the pain of looting and vandalism to have faded from his heart a bit. Even so, he was rarely so dismissive. After a moment, she logged into her computer and paged through her bookmarks. She tried not to make a habit of stalking the Founders, but times like this made her skin crawl with lack of information.

Their site was much the same: crimson and gold official weight lent by the website's .org suffix.

The crisp black letters emblazoned across the top designated it the home of Los Pobladores. She had once been drunk enough to read most of the testimonials regarding the archaeologists "raping the most ancient of Chilean history." She was too angry and too sober for that tonight. Instead, she flipped to the pictures of their protests. Right at the top were several of an achingly familiar valley. She had to admit, whoever they had snapping pictures was talented, a regular propaganda machine.

"What's up, Dirt-butt?" Mikey crouched on the fire escape, peering through the window. "I didn't hear voices, so I figured you hadn't gotten through to Martos."

"I called him yesterday, told him about the site. He called back but doesn't seem to think it's a big deal."

"That bother you?"

"It's been years since that man put a shovel in the ground. He probably forgets how much it gets to us."

Mikey climbed in and handed her the beer she had forgotten on the roof before popping the top of one of his own. "Whatcha looking at?" He peered at the screen and groaned. "Nel, no."

"Look, I needed to know for sure. They've protested us before, but this is way out of bounds. I wanted to know if they were owning it. Just look at this mess. Their shutter bug is damned good. Our crew look like privileged, soft Americans, you look like a grunt out of Lara Croft, and I look like...." She shoved the computer away.

Mikey took it from her carefully and flipped through the pictures, stone-faced. "You look angry, Nel, that's all. And I am, basically, a grunt. And the crew is mostly greens—soft and American. That's how we all start. There's nothing here that isn't true. We've got our funding, so what are you so worried about?"

"Honestly, I have no idea." She set her elbows on her knees, peeling at the label of her still-unopened beer. "In undergrad I was walking back to my dorm from the SU. There were a few street-lights on the path, but it was pretty dark—lots of trees. I got a third of the way through the green and felt like some electric shock went up my back. Way worse than any willies. I turned tail and ran back to the SU and called Jim—you know, Jim Halen—to give me a ride. Next day, turns out some poor girl was attacked by a creep on that same path."

"You've lost me, Nel." He put aside the computer and edged closer to her.

"I mean, I got the willies and listened to them."

"You're worried you're not listening to them now?"

"This whole situation feels the same as that path did. I'm scared someone's gonna get hurt." She glanced over at the site maps, the artifacts, the tiny collection that she hoped would answer her oldest question. "I'm a bit excited, though."

Mikey grinned. "There's my stubborn girl."

She flashed him a smile that fell short of her eyes. "There's a reason we've scared the Founders with this one, Mikey. And I want to find out why."

THREE

The metallic *kiss-sha* of the screens echoed across the site. Nel pulled her field book out to plot the next transect. Four rows labeled A-D and 12 columns number 1-12 comprised the grid. It was an archaeological version of battleship—drop a meter square unit and cross your fingers for diagnostic artifacts.

She pulled Mikey aside. "Keep an eye on Shiloh, she seems a bit overconfident."

Nel stopped by George's screen. "You finding anything?"

George propped the screen on one knee, boot planted on the growing mound of dirt underneath, a land-locked Captain Morgan. He opened his hand to show her a nice collection of flakes. "Ten chert, six of this other stuff."

"Good job. You said you wanted to ask me something?"

He grimaced. "Yeah." He flicked the dirt from the screen before leading her back to his unit. Nel climbed into it, brow furrowed. The soil was dry and dense, the color of perfectly made coffee. "What's up?"

"I think I screwed up." The boy pointed to the thick black band that slashed diagonally through the neat stripes of color. "The color's all wrong. I think I dragged my boot across it."

Nel grinned. "George, that wasn't you. Looks like a burrow."

"How do you mean?"

"You know stratigraphy, the stripes in the dirt?"

"Yeah."

"They're not just any old color. They get lighter the further you go because you're getting farther from organic stuff and closer to crumbled rock. The black-red fluff that has leaves and stuff, that's organics. After that, you have a mixture of that stuff and whatever's further down. The deepest we go is the next layer, which is sand or bedrock, maybe silt if it's a flood deposit, or sometimes clay. That stripe is from some animal digging a burrow and taking organics down with it. Tracking in the mud, you could say." She scraped the offending color with her trowel. "See how it goes in, it's not just a scuff mark."

He grinned. "Thanks! I got worried I screwed up everything."

"We can usually tell when something is from diggers or other people like looters or construction. The stripes are all mixed together, the top's the wrong texture, and half the time they leave ciggs and coins and trash underneath everything. The colors are kind of how we determine rough eras too." She rose with a groan. "Keep going down for another level or two, but if you don't find anything else we'll call this one quits."

She paused at the camp table and flipped through the finds pages for that day. "There's precious little here, Mikey."

"I know. I think we're just not deep enough though. That biface frag they pulled from the embankment was pretty deep."

"A17 and 19 are almost on top of C. If they start going deeper than that we'll have a whole 'nother set of issues." Her eyes narrowed. "Maybe I should drop a China trench."

Mikey snorted. "The noobies always love that."

Nel's first dig had dug a unit until they hit the bedrock to get a better idea of the soil composition and color. The students had joked that they were digging to China, and the name stuck. She pulled the maps out and unrolled the one already sporting a dozen hand-drawn corrections. "Where do you think would be best?"

Mikey leaned on the table, blunt finger tracing the semi-circle of positive units. "Maybe at the peak of this arc here. Like a few meters off, between Grid A and the line of shovel tests you wanted to put in."

Nel nodded and began collecting the necessary paper work. "You want to do a walk over, see what we can find?"

"Sure thing." He dumped his pack and grabbed a water bottle and the camera. "Be back in a bit."

Nel hummed an answer, already elbow deep in the opening notes of the unit paperwork. She loved mapping, but the other paperwork was something that twisted in her gut like a knife. *Why did I ever want to be a teacher? All it involves is paperwork.* Finally she tapped it into order.

She found the center of A Grid and hooked her tape on a corner nail before pacing out 10m. She could see outcroppings of bedrock in the hills and behind her, so the China trench wouldn't last too long, she hoped. She slipped in her earbuds and flicked on her walkman. Mikey teased her for being a hipster, but the truth was her Zune was more durable than any iPod. She cranked the volume, head bobbing to "Holy Horseshit Batman" as she laid in the unit. One gnarled finger held the tapes down where they crossed at 100 and 141cm. *And I thought I'd never use geometry.* She tapped in the second corner nail that held the string outlining the unit.

Mikey's hand on her shoulder startled an entirely too high yelp from her throat. She jerked the headphones out and whirled to glare at him. "Was I singing again?"

He snorted. "Not loud enough to bother anyone. I like Gym Class Heroes, though, so I didn't rightly mind." He jerked his head behind him. "I've got something for you to see."

"Let me finish this?"

"Yeah, it's not going anywhere." He crouched and held one end of the tape, watching as her eyes inspected the shape for tiny imperfections before she dropped the last nail. "It's crazy how this becomes second nature, eh?"

"Yeah, something that seemed so foreign and complex is like breathing." She tied off the bright pink string that denoted the boundary of the unit before rising with a groan. "Oi, Annie!" she called across the site. "Keep an eye for a second, gotta check something." She followed Mikey to the crest of the hill. "They probably think we're hooking up."

Mikey made a face. "I doubt they think that. I'm pretty sure George just figured out you were female."

"Kind of," she joked. "What did you find?"

"We did the walk-over in the middle of the growing season, there were a shit-ton of plants, remember?"

"Yeah we could barely get through half the site without a machete."

"Well I think I found something the bushes were hiding." He paused at the crest of the hill and pointed. A line of brown-pink boulders marched away from them, straight and orderly. Another line arced away at an angle, like a narrow funnel. Nel's eyes narrowed. "Huh. Old river bed?"

"Look at the stones. Half of them are scoria."

"Did you take pictures?"

"A few. Feel free to take more. You want to map it in?"

"Yeah, and drop a transect down the middle. See what it looks like under there."

"You think it's cultural?"

"I think it could be." She scuffed at the dirt with her boot, glaring through the sun at Mikey's find. "I also think I'm artifact-starved and would label your fresh shit in the bushes proof of occupation."

Mikey laughed softly. "Alright, well let's get China started and we can map this tomorrow."

"I take it the total station is fucking up again?" She nodded to the piece of survey equipment that seemed to cause more problems than it solved. When it worked, it allowed them to record the exact location of certain points.

He grimaced. "Yep. I've never had this much trouble with it before. Might be the ocean or the altitude or something."

Nel flipped open her compass. "Yeah, I think my compass has sand in it. This site will be the death of our high budget if we keep fucking up our tools." She glanced back to the site. Kat was finishing unit paperwork. Nel nodded toward him. "Get Kat started on China Trench, I'll finish up this."

She jogged over to the first line of rocks and snapped a picture before tugging her field book out of her pack and quickly sketching the boulders.

25

HOLMES

There were twenty-seven of them, all between 1 and 2 m in size. Blood surged through her limbs. This was what archaeology was about. *Leaving Africa, crossing Beringia, crossing the Atlanic, finding the Moon. And archaeologists searching for where we began.* Nel paced out the lines, marking particularly interesting rocks as she passed.

Humans were explorers, right down to the base of whatever they called a soul.

FOUR

The Jeep made a good show of complaining as it hauled itself up the roads. Spinning tires and a fair amount of slamming gears between first and second soothed Nel's inner badass-rebel. The crew had settled into a good dynamic, but 7:00 a.m. starts weren't anyone's friend, especially after a night of drinking. The ride was silent, those who had international data plans updating Facebook and Twitter while they still had signal.

The car roared over the crest of the hills, jostling back into the ruts. Nel smelled the smoke before they rounded the bend. *Fuck.* It was one thing to tell greens about vandalism, to explain the heartbreak and the anger. When they didn't see it, it was just a good story. Seeing it meant calls to parents, and inevitably Nel would get phoned and emailed about safety.

She slowed the car and fumbled with the walkie-talkie that connected the Wrangler with

Mikey's Neon. "You smell that? Over." She was too worried to use their silly call-signs.

She watched his mouth thin in the rear-view mirror, pressing all expression from his face. "It'll look worse if we keep it from them. Over." She sighed and turned in her seat. "Alright, you all smell that smoke? I'm sure you've heard the worst about the site's condition our first day back this season. Looks like we got hit again. Phones away and keep your eyes and ears open. The vandals aren't violent, but they obviously lit something on fire—let's use our heads here. If the smoke's really bad, wet a bandana and put it over your face."

Nel watched in the rear-view until everyone had pocketed their phones and looked suitably alert. She slid the Jeep around the bend. Oily, black smoke billowed from the ground. Nel parked as far away as their site boundary allowed and climbed down. "Unload the water. We can bug out for lunch to get more." She snapped pictures, noting absently how steady her hands were around the warm metal of the camera.

"We got this, too, Dr. Bently." Annie held up the mini extinguisher.

"That's a last resort. I want stuff tested, not destroyed." She heard the mean edge to her voice, the low rumble that bordered on a sneer. She hoped the girl understood. Two minutes and an entire cooler of their drinking water later, the fire smoldered sullenly, but low enough for Nel to examine closer. Rotting pieces of some animal—

she would bet a goat, though it seemed to have died weeks ago—formed a symbol that they had then drenched in accelerant and ignited. *It's their goddamned logo.* "They sacrificed a damn goat and blazed their symbol in fire across my site, Mikey." Her voice was low enough so only he could hear.

"Sacrificed? That's not their style."

"OK, not sacrificed. The thing looks like it was butchered—like, for food—several weeks ago. Probably off of someone's trash heap."

He rested a hand on her shoulder. To the crew it looked like a pat on the back. Truly, it was a firm anchor while her mind whirled in a roiling sea of anger. "I'll take some pictures and clean this up. We need to open C-transect today."

She nodded once, then twice, finally clearing her throat and rubbing her palms together. "Alright gang. Mikey will take care of this. Everyone else, get caught up on paperwork, fill out your artifact tracking sheets, and we'll go through the typology book together." Her voice was a distant sound through the rage roaring in her ears.

"I feel like shit, Mikey."

"What's up?" He eased into the porch seat beside her, adjusting his shorts before leaning back.

Nel softened a moment. Mikey was good at listening. Anyone else would assume why she was upset and rattle a litany of advice and optimism at her. *Mikey, though, he's got empathy down to a fucking science.* "Well, I'm angry about the vandalism, obviously, but I also have this level of guilt. This is their land. I can't pretend it's not. This is their home. As hard as I try, I can't pretend I belong here. I've met these people's children, eaten their food, but I don't know them. Part of me feels like I have no reason to be upset."

"I feel you. It's hard, coming down here. We've got a different language, different backgrounds. I could pass as Hispanic, but hell, you're a different color. That makes it look even worse if someone wants to pick. I think you're seeing things, though."

Nel sighed. "Really?"

"Yeah. You got the permits. You didn't hire locals for the manual labor, and the times you have you haven't paid them a pittance. There's very little gentleman explorer about you." He reached over and patted her hand. "I know it doesn't make you feel any better, but I think you're safe from being tossed onto the bigot train."

Nel laughed. "I very much would like to avoid the bigot train. With the kinds of people on it, I'd never get laid."

Mikey grinned. "Nonsense, I know plenty of racist lesbians. Plus, you wouldn't have to go far to start bunking together. It'd be a dream come true."

Nel snorted. "Not every lesbian moves in on the second date."

"Really? Which ones?"

"The ones who got fucked over the last time they ran instead of walked." She stuck her tongue out at him. After a moment she glanced over. "When do you think you'll find someone?"

"Maybe I don't want to."

"I know you do. You like having a warm bed and someone to talk to. Half the time we talk it's because you're lonely."

He shrugged, dark eyes narrowing in thought. He scrubbed a hand over his short hair. "I don't know. There's no one on the horizon. I think I need to be in a different place. This job doesn't suit monogamy."

"You're telling me." Nel reached over and took his big hand in hers, turning it over to look at the dark patches of callus. "She's going to be tall and curvy. She'll have a good job, something selfless, but she'll drink you under the table. You'll meet in a bar and she'll be swaying to Hozier or George Ezra."

Mikey snorted, eying her with wounded humor. "You a palmist now?"

"Hardly, I just know what you look for."

He grinned and leaned back, staring at the stars. "I'm glad I have you, at least. You make it easier."

"Make what easier?"

He shrugged. "You're going to find someone badass and driven, someone who runs as fast as you do, and suddenly you'll realize you're running in the same direction."

Nel made a show of snuggling into the chair. "Oh, do tell me more, Uncle Mikey! Will she have legs for days?"

"If you want." He laughed softly, the weight of the day dissolving as his laughter tumbled from him in a gentle cascade. He squeezed her hand as the mirth faded slightly from his face. "Living, Nel. You make living easier."

She turned away, following his gaze to the stars. His loneliness was contagious sometimes, but she enjoyed the emotion and nostalgic melancholy. He didn't. She squeezed his hand back. "You make everything easier too."

FIVE

Sun-fired soil crunched under Nel's boots. It was almost surprising when there was no vandalism. Perhaps they stayed out late the night before, and were too hung over to trash her site. She opened her field book, changing the partners around. She glanced up as Mikey's shadow fell over her. "Alright, get Henri set with those two units, then I want you running the total station for this."

Mikey rolled his eyes. "I've got to re-calibrate it, but it'll be ready when you are."

The battered yellow case of the total station was something more common for DOT road surveys, but it was worth its considerable weight in platinum. Nel started doing the walkover, eyes glued to the ground. The sounds of hard earth and metal and the buzz of insects were a favorite song. She never grew sick of it. The western end of the site was normal enough—the roughly semi-circular layout faced south-east, toward the river and backed against the windbreak of the hills. It was the eastern part that bothered her. She frowned at the unusual landform. It was too flat and too straight for anything natural, even a flood. *Besides, it would have flooded west, into the ocean.* Instead, it widened to the east, a great flat, long funnel.

She paced along the northernmost edge. It was bordered by rocks, large ones that would have been hard to move. *As if the landform wasn't odd enough.* She sketched the rough shape of the wall, following it until it petered out several hundred meters away from the site. She turned around, stepped a few paces from her last path, and walked back. Walkovers were meditative and having real eyes—not a camera or a fly-by's aerial shots—was always best. The human eye saw things nothing else would. On her first survey, someone found a point—rich black obsidian with a green vein. The knapper had shaped it in a way that made the green run straight down the center of the point. Humans were nothing if not artistic. If she liked the shape of a hill, it was likely someone fifteen thousand years before would have too.

"Nel, all set!" Mikey jogged over with the total station pole—a red-and-white striped staff with a prism set at the top. It looked uncannily like a wizard's rod from Magic the Gathering.

Mikey handed it to her, his features schooled into practiced sobriety. "With great power, comes great responsibility."

Nel grinned at his quote and took the staff. One day she would figure out how much of their conversations were just repeated annually. She guessed more than half. "I'll write the points, you record the coordinates, K?" When he nodded, she headed to the nearest corner and planted the steel point at the top of the first rock. She stared absently at the level bubble. She could do this in her sleep. She moved down the line, choosing the largest rocks or those from non-local sources. It took two hours to record the entire formation, and by the time she was done, her eyes hurt from the sun and her crew had already taken lunch. She trudged back and perched on one of the boulders at the side, copying Mikey's coordinates into her field book.

She stared at the drawing, brows knotted and half of a smashed sandwich forgotten in her hand.

"Nel, we're packing it in, you good to go?"

She glanced up. "What?" The sun was low and the crew looked as tired as she felt. "Shit, yeah sorry." She tossed her tools and the paperwork into her pack and pulled herself back onto the jeep. "You got the finds?"

Mikey nodded. "Got some good ones today. Might even be some diagnostics in there."

She grinned. "That's what I like to hear."

There was a third upstairs bedroom, across from the bathroom, that held the artifacts and maps, anything too precious for the Jeep or the site. Finally clean, and with a cold beer in hand, Nel pulled out the day's bag of artifacts and propped the door open with a brick. A tiny portable speaker muttered out Shing02, and Nel upended the bag over the desk. Every level of every quad of every unit received its own bag for chipping debris. Nel went through each, washing the smooth stone and re-bagging it. It was tedious work, but meditative and something she preferred to do alone, or at least without conversation. She washed the chipping debris and placed it into a cataloging box. Only the tools were left. Each had their own, double bag, complete with a packet of soil. Tools were diverse across location and time periods, and much could be determined from their shape and material.

The advent of microscopes, however, had brought a slew of new information. Tiny nicks on the edge of blades and points, invisible to the naked eye, could determine the material on which the tool had been used. Protein analysis would tell, sometimes within a genus, what meat may have been cut.

Granted, if a crewmember touched the tool, analysis would be just as likely to pick up their own protein or that of the roast beef sandwich they had for lunch. Many of the tools weren't pretty— fragmented or of poor-quality material that degraded easily. The crew found two point types on the site. The first was the broad fishtail, the other Clovis-style fluted points. The second had a channel knocked from the center of the base to help wedge the stone into a split spear shaft. The combination of the two wasn't common for younger sites, but Nel grinned. *This site is old, then.* The controversy of Monte Verde made any archaeologist leery of ambiguous data from the region, but Nel was confident this site wouldn't cause any paradigm shifts.

Someone knocked softly and pushed open the door. "Hey, Dr. Bently, can I talk to you?"

Nel glanced up. Annie stood in the doorway, shifting from foot to foot. "Of course, everything okay?" Nel was no stranger to crew drama, but it was not high on her list of favorite things. She reached over and paused her music before leaning back in the chair. "What's up?"

Annie perched on a chair opposite her. "I'm kind of worried about the looting. And I don't know what to do with my career."

"Those sound like distinct issues."

"I guess. Maybe. The first class I took with you, I decided I wanted to be you when I graduated. Like, I wanted to run my own site and all. But with the looting and seeing how angry it makes you and how you handle things, it makes me think I couldn't handle the same thing."

Nel frowned. "That's flattering, Annie, thank you. I think your worries are good concerns to have at this point. Archaeology isn't an easy field. We snipe at each other, it's a small world, and burning bridges is very easy. The hours are long and the travel is tough and the weather can suck. What is your favorite part of this job? Is it the learning or the digging?"

Annie shrugged. "I guess the digging. I like working outside and I like the methodical work and the idea that we're allowing people to know more. I mean, school is great, but I don't ever want to teach."

Nel grinned. "You're done with classes. All that's left is your thesis. Try CRM—cultural resource management. It's all digging and no teaching. Many places will take you with just an undergrad, so you'd be golden."

"I just don't know where to start."

"Tell you what, let's get through this season. When we get back I'll make some calls. I know people who might need help on their crews." She watched Annie's face a moment. "Is there anything else bothering you?" When the girl shook her head, Nel pushed a bag towards her. "I've got some artifacts from yesterday that need washing and cataloging. Wanna help?"

Annie grinned and scooted closer. "Do we have to listen to angry Japanese rap?"

Nel snorted, "No, but whatever you put on damn well better not be Top 40."

SIX

Mikey heaved himself on to the barstool next to her. "You know, this place has all kinds."

"What makes you say that?"

"There's this girl, met her down at the grocer's. She's got this whole idea of bringing chocolate to the states."

"I'm pretty sure we have chocolate in the states. I wouldn't have lived through my teen years if we didn't"

"No one would have lived through your teen years, Nel. But, no, I mean *real* chocolate. Like, the beans roasted and ground and all that. She wants to set up shop near her hometown."

"Yeah, where's she from?"

"Petersburg or something."

"That's in Russia," Nel reminded him.

"I'm sure there's more than one. Anyways, I thought I'd help her with backing when she gets it more underway."

"For sure, that sounds interesting. Always good for people to know the origins and processes of their food."

Mikey turned to her, waving a motherly finger. "Speaking of which, you were up late last night—you went out?"

"No, just looking over the site maps. Something isn't setting well with me. The layout, it's not like the other paleo sites."

"It's your oldest one so far, right?"

"Based on lithics, yeah. I'd like to get some dates though."

"Those dates are so vague, the margin of error is hundreds of human generations. When you're determining when these folks lived, that's a big difference."

"Makes the money-bags happy though." Nel stretched. "Seriously though, the shape is all wrong. That big flat plain and everything—it's weird."

"Maybe they had a flood."

"Mikey, there are no alluvial sands, no flood strats, no clay."

He tipped back his beer. "Well, you worry about strats, I'll worry about chocolate. We're opening up another two trenches, right?"

"Yeah, tomorrow. I was going to put George and Sally on A21 and Henri and Kat on B20."

"Sally's banging George. Might wanna shake that up a bit."

Nel groaned. It was archaic to think sex would change people's working habits, especially in a field with rampant hook-ups and drinking. Still, undergrads had less experience being professional. "Seriously? Every time I make a perfect crew someone has to get randy."

"I'm just surprised. He could do better than Sal."

"Standards aren't as big a deal. It's sex, not a binding contract."

"Well, for some of us they're the same thing."

"I'm so glad I never slept with you."

"I think I lack the appropriate number of tits and have one too many dicks for you."

Nel glanced over, eyeing him up and down. The yellow light of the bar cast his tan into a rich brown. He wasn't half bad, for a guy, but she hadn't been with a man in close to a decade. Mikey certainly wasn't how she was going to break that streak. "If you keep eating homemade chocolate, you might have bigger boobs than me."

Mikey shoved her off her stool playfully. "That's not hard, shovel-bum." He frowned suddenly. "Speaking of trowels for hire, you hear Chad's coming in?"

Nel frowned. "What? When? Why?"

"Martos apparently called in a favor and got him transferred here, full pay. Our funder asked for another set of eyes—not because yours are lacking, but to help."

Nel shrugged. "Chad won't step on any toes, even if he's asked to. He's a good guy, it'll be nice to see him again. Curious what exactly they want, though."

"You can ask him yourself by the end of the week."

Nel rose with a groan. "I'm going to turn in. Last night's catching up with me." She dropped a wad of crumpled bills on the bar. "Don't stay up too late." She waved and headed out into the balmy night air. The air was the same temperature as her skin. A soft wind that she could barely feel raised the hairs on her arm. She grinned. As much as anyplace, this was home.

She broke into a jog, enjoying the feeling of hot blood pumping through her legs. She was tired, but not ready to return to the house just yet, despite what she had told Mikey. She turned right and followed a private road towards the hills. It was a longer walk overland, but far more pleasant. She slowed to a walk where it ended and climbed past the quiet rows of houses and into the hills on the southern edge of the town.

The lights below were a tiny golden galaxy in the warm black of the landscape. Beyond, the moon spilled a white staircase across the dimpled ocean surface. She was passing Padritos when she heard gravel crunch. She paused, but the sound stopped. The moonlight yielded nothing behind her, save for the spindly silhouetted trees. She continued along the crest of the hill, steps quiet despite her boots.

The footsteps followed her, an echo to her own, just off enough to send awareness skittering up her spine.

Another minute's walk brought her within sight of the house. The steps quickened with her own. She broke into a run, stumbling down the slope into the sanctuary of the flood lamp buzzing by the back porch. Cold, dry fingers brushed down her neck. A scream bubbled in her throat, bitten by her clenched teeth. Her hand found the doorknob.

She did not take the time to look before bursting into the hall and slamming the door behind her. She slid down it, legs and hands shaking. *I just imagined it.* Still, she didn't look out. When her heart was steady again she moved quietly upstairs. It was the first time in years she locked her bedroom door. Despite the beautiful breeze, she slammed her window and slid the lock home.

She perched on her bed, scrolling through webcomics and news articles until well after midnight, unable to sleep.

The next morning, Nel climbed into the hills before breakfast. The bright sun burned away last night's fear and glinted off the ocean in the distance. She paced along the ridge, eyes narrowed on her tracks from the night before. Gnawing dread chased away the sun's warmth. Another set of boot prints followed hers down the hill. They circled the building before disappearing onto the asphalt of the road. There was a deep impression at the side of the building where someone had waited for several minutes. Nel glanced up. They stopped directly below her window.

SEVEN

The rumble of heavy treads on dirt heralded Chad's arrival several minutes before his Land Rover trundled to a stop beside their vehicles. He swung out, waving a tanned hand at her before reaching into the back to grab his field pack.

Nel jogged over with a smile. "Hey, Paleo-man!"

"Hey, Cave-woman." His hug was tight and exactly what she needed after Monday. "Looks like you've got a lot of work done."

"A fair amount. We've got a shovel-test transect headed east. You said you missed contract work, I thought you could help them."

"Show me the maps and I'll jump in."

Nel beckoned Annie over. "You just finished B3, right?" When she nodded, Nel pointed to the line of squares drawn between the rocks. "I want to you do this transect. Annie, you remember Chad?"

Annie smiled and offered her hand. "You were on site two years ago?"

"Yep. Good to see you." Chad shook her hand before tying a faded bandana around his black hair.

Nel handed Annie a stack of shovel-test paperwork. "Do true 50cm squares and don't stop until you're 10cm into the C, regardless of what you find."

"Why're we doing this? Determine the boundary of the site?"

Nel glanced out at the stones. "Yeah." She didn't want them biased to find something and two lines of rocks were nothing to get a grad student excited about yet. "Let me know if you get anything weird, and please don't lump any strats—there might be alluvial deposits."

Annie trotted off to grab a round shovel and screen.

Nel tossed Chad a bundle of artifact bags and tags with a bright smile. "Here, I hope you need these."

Chad caught them and bent over the map. "What are these rocks? You're not checking the boundary of the site, you're testing those."

"Fuck if I know. I just don't want her getting excited."

"If you don't trust her, why are you letting her do this?"

"She's fast and thorough, but not confident."

Chad's dark brows rose. "None of us were, Nel. She's got to start somewhere."

"Can I talk to you?" Mikey leaned out of his doorway as Nel climbed the stairs to their rooms.

She unlocked her door and edged in. "Yeah, come on in."

"No, I need you to actually listen."

Nel frowned. *That sounds ominous.* She dropped her pack in her room and crossed the hall to his. It was messy, but lacked the distinct war-zone feel of hers. "What's up?"

Mikey sat on the edge of his bed. "You've got to handle the students better."

"What do you mean?"

"I mean you need to teach them."

She frowned. Mikey rarely got so earnest, but if there was one thing he took seriously, it was education. "It's field school, Mikey, I am teaching them."

"Really? Because the past week I've watched you snap twice at Sally, blatantly take something out of Henri's hands to do it yourself without clarification, and you've only explained the whys of things on a need-to-know basis."

"This site is weird. I don't want to confuse them."

"Dammit, Nel, they're adults—this is what they want to do for a living. Part of field school is learning what to do when the weird stuff happens.

I want you to do your damn job. Say what's going on or why you don't know. I want you to explain things before you have to. You shouldn't be waiting for them to mess up and then correcting them. You should show them the proper way."

Nel's stomach was in knots. She hated when Mikey was mad at her. He was so patient that when he lost his temper it was closer to disappointment than anger. Disappointment felt far worse on the receiving end. "Mikey, we approach things differently. I'm a throw-you-in kind of person."

"This is why Martos questioned whether you should run the school at all this year. You can't even accept the fact that you've been an ass to half of them. At other field schools, the teachers and students eat together every night. They're so terrified of dealing with you we only see them one night a week."

Nel rose. "Are you done? Because I'm not up to listening to you tear me down right now."

"Neither were they."

She slammed the door behind her and stalked into the bathroom. She jerked the curtain closed and turned the water on hot. *I'll take the longest shower of the season and he'll deal with cold water.*

Nel's boots thumped against the bar stool rungs. Violetta Parra was not her favorite musician, and her music in this bar felt a bit too fitting. Still, the rhythm got under her skin. Songs with good rhythm were the heartbeat of an archaeologist. *The pounding of shovels on dirt echoes in our favorite music.*

Dirt was the reason Nel breathed, the reason her feet walked, the reason she grinned even after a shit day.

"Buy you a drink?"

Nel turned. The owner of Padritos perched on the stool next to her. His face was written in contrasts. The expression was open but belied the unfathomed depths in his dark eyes. The faint lines in his face deepened as his brows inched upwards.

"Ah, Emilio, was it?"

"Yeah."

She shifted. This was easy in the States, but she had never had to actually come out while in Chile. She assumed the locals were less than interested in her looks. "Ah, you're not quite what I go for, Emilio." She slipped into her serviceable Spanish.

He snorted. "And you aren't what I go for. Buying you a drink doesn't mean I want in your sheets. It means you seem interesting."

She grinned. "Alright, a gin and tonic then." She shifted towards him. Though they ate at his place almost every week during the season, she knew little about him. "Did you grow up here?"

"Born and raised. My family has lived on this land forever."

She raised her brows. Most of the locals drifted in from larger towns when they grew too crowded. The discovery of Mont Verde brought in enough tourists to the south, but this was still a hidden gem. "Your family open the restaurant or was that you?"

"My brother, actually. When he died I took over."

"I'm sorry to hear. What did you do before that?"

He held up a finger and nodded at the music. "These are my favorite words of hers:
...el arco de las alianzas ha penetrado en mi nido con todo su colorido, se ha paseado por mis venas..."

He hummed the next line then turned back to her with a smile. "I worked for the government—roads, survey, and so forth. The restaurant is nice, but I miss being outside. You come here for the archaeology?"

"I did." The subject of her studies often met with mixed opinions. "I study the first people here."

"The Mapuche? You don't like the Aztec? Or the Conquistadors?"

"I think the Aztec were phenomenal—very advanced. Conquistadors were less so. I started with the Mapuche, but the older the better. I like simple times, simple lives, and you look back far enough, to when we only worried about food and shelter, I think you learn a lot about what humans are."

He nodded sagely. "I see. You want to know about who we were, who we are."

"I guess. I think to understand where we're going, we need to know where we've been." She had written an entire essay on why she dug. It was difficult to articulate, but the search for self was high on her list of reasons.

"I think every part of our lives is one long search for home. I think true humanity comes from that search, the understanding that everyone searches."

"You're a smart one, Emilio." She nudged him. "I think we should have gone for drinks a long time ago."

"Perhaps. I was a different man three years ago. I used to think that humanity was the search for the future—building roads, building ourselves up, growing greater and greater, and dreaming of all we could be. The 'where we're going' you spoke of. Now I know I was wrong."

"How so?"

"That is not the right of it. That is the path to losing our humanity. We break ourselves when we build too high. The tree cannot be mighty without the roots, if you pardon the metaphor."

Nel shrugged. "We must agree to disagree then. I think our greatest achievements have been through leaping, untethered. Certainly look back, but leaping is when we grow."

"And what have you discovered, in your leaping? Anything on your site that tells you where to leap?"

She laughed. "It's a nice site, but nothing spectacular. We've got mostly Jack and Shit, and Jack left town."

His laugh was low and rolling, the sound of a storm too far to feel the rain. "Well, I wish you luck."

She grinned. "And I hope you find your roots."

"Why do you think I haven't already?"

"Because you said it was the search that gave us humanity."

His eyes crinkled deeper. "Here, let us take a picture together—for the wall of my restaurant. I can say the famous archaeologist ate here every summer. The crowds will come from miles."

She rolled her eyes and pulled her best plastic grin on while he fumbled his camera phone out and leaned in. His shoulder was warm and hard from work. The faux shutter clacked and he sat back. "Good."

She knocked back her drink. "I think I better walk this off before morning. Thanks for the talk."

"Thank you as well. I'll see you next week?"

"Sure thing." Quiet and cool washed over her as she stepped out onto the porch. The air was just shy of warm, but the waves in the distance would be comfortable. As a rule, Nel didn't often join the crew on their various excursions, whether they were drinking, eating, or swimming. She was good at faking, but at the end of the day, she wasn't a people person. "I prefer my people buried bones." The words crackled in the perfect loneliness of the night.

She thrust her hands into her pockets and trudged down the road towards the ocean. She perched on a rock to unlace her boots. The coarse sand felt smooth under her rough feet, and within a minute her clothes were a forgotten pile. The Pacific was cold for only a moment, the discomfort erased by a laughing yelp. The salt water lifted her, echoing the weightlessness of space, the buoyancy before birth. Her eyes found the Southern Cross in the sky, and she struck out, arms propelling her into colder, deeper waters. *We might need our roots, but only as reminders. It was a leap that brought humans to the Americas—across Beringia, across the Atlantic and Pacific. It will be a leap that carries us to Mars, to other as yet unnamed worlds.* She flipped onto her back, swimming a tiny metaphor for the belief twisted deep in her heart.

EIGHT

Chad jogged over to where Nel crouched in one of the units. "Hey, want to take a look at this?"

She rose with a groan. "Sure. What's up?"

"We got a weird strat. And I checked out those rocks earlier. You know they're all hematite?"

She grabbed his hand and let him pull her out of the block. "I didn't. I'll have to note that. How many pits have you done?"

"Half. First one looked like these, but the last five have been strange. They have this lens of black shit. Thought you'd want to check it out."

Nel grabbed her field book and began sketching the numbers for a profile map. "How deep have you gone?"

"80 on average. Lens is at 40cm."

Nel frowned. "That's right in the middle of our occupation."

"Yep." Chad crouched beside their second pit. "This is where it came in. It's thin here, but levels out around 2cm thick in the last one."

Nel glanced at Annie. "Mind if I check it out?"

Annie stepped back with a headshake.

Nel jerked her trowel out of her side pocket and crouched at the edge of the pit. She scraped the inside of the wall roughly, exposing fresh stratigraphy. She hummed thoughtfully, brows twisted. "You found anything?"

"Nothing in the way of tools," Chad answered. "A few flakes in the first two, but not much compared to the others."

"Dr. Bently? There's a sheen to that layer, like there's mica or something." Annnie pointed to the strata.

Nel's gaze flicked to Annie. She had forgotten the girl was there. "Good eye. You think it's shiny like silt? You know, when you kick up the bed of a stream?"

Annie lifted a shoulder in a shrug. "I don't think so. Hard to say in these, though, it's easier to get an idea for that in the units. It doesn't seem dark enough for charcoal, though, so it's not a fire feature."

Nel surprised herself with a smile. "Alright, keep going with this line. Let me think about what I want to do with it. Maybe a unit or two would be a good idea, Annie."

Nel opened the screen door and poked her head out. Annie sat in one of the chairs, an e-reader held in one hand, a lemonade in the other. "Mind if I join you?"

Annie glanced up then shook her head. "I just wanted some fresh air. Not a lot of air moving and my room's like a hot-box."

Nel slid into the chair opposite the girl, slouching with her legs splayed. She hated awkward talks. "What are you reading?"

"*How to get Arrested* by Cameron J Quinn."

"Haven't read it."

"It's a paranormal novella-thing, like Buffy grown up."

"Cool." Nel lapsed into silence. She loved reading, but paranormal wasn't her style. A dark thriller or crime was good on a winter day. She looked at the clouds then at the balcony when a door slammed upstairs. After counting the number of flowers on the vines along the rail for the second time, she leaned forward. "Can I talk to you?"

Annie's face blanched and she flicked the e-reader off. "Yeah. What did I do?"

"No, it's nothing you did, Annie. That's kind of the point." Nel shifted again. "I suck at this. Um, here's the thing about women and archaeology— we're strong and smart and rough. We know what it takes to cut it in a man's world and how to take care of ourselves. We get used to giving no quarter and that makes for pretty shitty friendships between one another."

"Are you hitting on me?"

Nel stuttered on her next prepared line. "Shit, no, Annie. You're my student!"

Annie shrugged. "I'm sorry, I didn't mean to presume. I just have no idea what you're getting at."

You and me both, kid. "What I'm trying to say— badly apparently—is that I've been a shit to you. I'm not good at nurturing, and I'm as hard on my students and my diggers as my teachers were on me. This isn't an easy field and we've got to be tough. Sometimes I take that a little too far, though. You're not going to learn, or have any confidence, if I don't tell you when you're right as well as wrong."

"Oh." Annie fiddled with the hem of her jeans. "I think I get it. I just thought you didn't want to be a teacher or I was a bad student."

Nel looked down. "It's not easy for me, but I love field schools. You're not bad—you're one of the best archaeologists I have out here. I paired you with Chad because I know you won't learn anything with the others. You're good enough to work with him and I trust you enough with something unusual."

Annie's face lit up. "Really?"

"Yeah. You're gonna be one of the good ones, you just have to trust that. I guess, so do I." She patted the chair arms. "Alright, well, I'll see you tomorrow." She rose abruptly and ducked back into the house. Chad leaned on the counter, grinning, as she stepped inside.

"You've got a way with words."

Nel glowered at him. "Seriously? She thought I was asking her out."

"Yeah, but what you said was actually really nice and honest. I never think of being hard on each other because you're women, but I guess it's true."

She pulled up a stool across from him. "Yeah, it can get really bad." She heaved a sigh. "You think Mikey's still mad at me?"

"I think he could never be mad at you for long."

She shrugged. "I never know why, though. He's so kind and then there's me. I don't get why he's been my friend for so long when I'm this prickly."

The needle hovered at north, minute trembles compensating for the slightest shifting in Nel's hand. Her engineer's sighting compass was old, older than herself. The hard black case was scratched and faded.

"Hey."

She refused to turn around at Mikey's voice. Her eyes narrowed on the north arrow.

He sighed softly and swung his leg over the wall to sit beside her. "I know you're angry. I deserve that." His gaze fell to the compass. "Is it that? You only look at that thing when you're really upset."

"It's my dad's. He gave it to me when I came out."

"That's not what I was asking."

"You said I was a shitty teacher."

He looked down at his hands. "I know. I'm sorry. It's a sensitive subject for me and I said some things I really shouldn't have."

"Do you actually think that, though?"

"I think you could be better, but you're not bad. Teaching isn't easy, especially in such a politically charged field."

Nel jerked a single nod at him. "This is the most reliable compass I have. Why doesn't it work at our site?"

"Can we talk about this, please? I hate when we fight."

Nel sighed and clicked her compass closed. "Alright."

"My first year of undergrad there was this teacher I admired so much. He was energetic and seemed to know everything there was to know. When I looked at him, I saw who I wanted to be. I took every class of his I possibly could. He was the worst grader I've ever seen. He never once admitted my verbal answers were right. He would only point out the details I'd missed. I spent three semesters thinking I was stupid. Finally, I went to get him to sign off on the paperwork for switching my major from Archaeology to Education. He asked why, and I told him I wasn't smart enough for it. 'Michael, you're one of the brightest students I have,' he said. He proceeded to explain that he was trying to push me. I lost it. I had grown to hate the man and in turn hate the part of me that still wanted to be him." He glanced over at Nel. "I'm sorry what I said hurt you."

Nel eyed him. "I get it. I am a shitty teacher sometimes. I forget people learn differently. It's hard to remember how vulnerable we all were in undergrad."

"Sometimes I see you being hard on your students and I worry."

"I always assume they can take it, that they're strong and smart because they've gotten this far. I forget that everyone has bad days and sometimes you just can't deal."

Mikey nudged her shoulder with his. "There you go. I never want someone to hate you."

Nel glanced over. *He yelled at me because he doesn't want a student to hate me.* "You're perfect, you know. A perfect fucking human."

NINE

"Dr. Bently!" The shout echoed across the site. Nel rubbed the bridge of her nose. All she really wanted was to finish the maps. "One second, Henri!" She rotated the protractor and made a mark to designate the location of the newest open unit. *A few dozen flakes, a base or tip here and there.* It was precious little for a site so perfect. Finally she rolled the map up again and rose with a groan. Henri crouched in the 1 meter square pit to the north of B-grid. His frown curled his unruly black brows together.

"What's up?"

Henri sat back on his heels and pointed with the tip of his trowel. "I think I got something."

A sharp edge of rock jutted a centimeter above the surface of the level. It was a rich red brown. "I think it's a point."

Nel grinned. Diagnostics always got her going. "I think you're right." She jogged back to her pack and found the tupperware she used for her smaller excavation tools. She nudged Mikey with the steel toe of her boot. "Henri's got something. Gather the gang."

She crouched at the edge of the unit. "Did you touch it with your hands?" When Henri shook his head she handed him a set of nitrile gloves. "Put these on. Excavate it carefully and pop it in this bag." She laid out a clean artifact bag and paper envelope. "Once you're through, record where it was—distance from the south and west walls and its depth." His speed, or lack thereof, exasperated Nel, but this time she was glad he was so meticulous. *Tell them what they do right.* She cleared her throat. "I'm glad you were the one to find this. You're very careful, and I know you'll do it properly."

Henri glanced up with a quiet smile before turning back to his task. When the rest of the diggers arrived Nel reiterated her instructions. "The gloves protect the tool from the protein on our bodies. We'll send it to be tested for protein residue. It'll tell us what the tool was used on." Her gaze swiveled back to Henri.

After several minutes of careful picking, Henri cleaned away enough soil that the rock was perched on a pedestal of dirt. He tipped the potential tool carefully into a gloved hand and held it up with a triumphant smile. "What do you think of that, Dr. Bently?"

She quickly tugged on a set of gloves and brushed the rest of the remaining dirt away from the stone. The spear point was almost as long as her hand, the flaking curving in from the razor edge. *I bet Mikey could shave off his beard with this.* The stone was a rich golden brown. "This is fucking beautiful." She held it up for the others to see. "Gang we got a perfect diagnostic! Dinner and drinks on me at Padrito's tonight!"

Chile pepper and corn flour wafted from the open wall of the restaurant. Music and the smell of food and ocean were the layered paint beneath the artwork of the night. Nel shoved her hands into her pockets. The diggers trailed after her loudly, attention turned inward.

Chad sidled up to her. "This one's tough on you, huh?"

She made a face.

His eyes were kind, but pointed. "Why do you think Martos sent me here? Is it just Los Pobladores?"

"It's complicated, Chad." She sighed. "First thing I saw when I set boots on the soil was a trashed site. That's not 'just' anything."

"They've trashed you before."

She glared at him, but there was no venom in the expression. "You're still in the field. You have no excuse to think vandalism is anything less than shitty."

"You're right. It's been a while since I've seen it, though, and it's never been my site. Looters still piss me off. They take anything?"

"Nothing. They didn't even fuck the strats up."

"That's bizarre. They told you why they care?"

"Other than the this-is-our-land-get-off part, no. But the thing is they've never claimed these sites to be their ancestors' before. I don't know why they suddenly started."

He wrapped an arm around her shoulders with a sigh. "I don't know either, Nel."

She stepped aside with him as he held open the restaurant door for the crew. "I don't really want to dwell on it, alright? Let's just tell war stories for the noobies."

"Deal." He grinned.

The tables at the back were already pushed together for them. Nel slid into a corner seat, letting Chad take the head. She scanned the specials absently as the others settled around the table and poured drinks. She didn't really need the menu—she had memorized it by the second week last year. It was her favorite restaurant in the area and was worth the price. Besides, Emilio always made a point of checking in with their table. "Don't worry about drinks, we'll grab some at the bar later, if you want to join us."

"I'm sure they'll go out to the club." Mikey reminded.

The awkward chuckles were enough of an answer and Nel shrugged. "Suit yourselves, just remember the morning comes early."

"You're one to talk." Chad responded. "Let's get the chapalele and the empanadas to share."

"Awesome." Nel folded her menu and leaned forward. Conversation slowed and the students' eyes turned to her. "How many archaeologists does it take to screw in a light bulb?" It was a joke from a coworker back when Nel had done CRM and it was her personal favorite.

Their heads shook, slightly bewildered stares passing between them. Annie leaned back, a slight smile playing across her mouth. "How many, Dr. Bently?"

Nel's coy smile curled into a wicked one. "An infinite amount—one to screw in the bulb and all the rest to talk about how, one time, they screwed in a bigger bulb under worse conditions."

Chad snorted into his beer and after a moment the rest of the crew began to laugh.

"They'll figure out the truth soon enough, Chadley." Mikey chuckled. "Seriously, it never gets old."

Henri glanced over. "Chadley? Is that your full name?"

Chad's brows rose. "I had this tradition, see, when I worked in offices. I'd learn who the most gossipy person was, and when we were alone doing a project, I'd confide that my name was not actually Chad."

"What is it?"

"My name is actually Chad. I'd tell them my name was Chadley, but I hated it so much that I never used it. I'd ask them to keep it quiet then watch over the next few weeks as the rumor of 'Chadley' circulated through the entire office."

"Whatever for?"

"Boredom, what else," Mikey interjected. "There's a reason why he works the field now."

Chad rolled his eyes and pulled a cigarette from the pack rolled into his shirtsleeve. "I liked tracking the gossip. You tell one, Wise-guy."

Mikey shrugged. "I had a fairly tame career. I'm making up for it by working with Nel."

Nel rolled her eyes and threw her napkin at him.

"The past two years have been the most lively yet." He swatted Nel's projectile away and raised his hand in surrender. "Okay. There was this one site during undergrad. It was out in the boonies and was super windy. There were these wild goats everywhere. One night there was a storm, and when we got to the site the next day, there were all these dead goats that had been blown off the cliff and onto our site. There was one in my unit even."

"Bullshit," Nel accused.

"Honest to God."

"You're atheist." Nel pointed to the bottle of table wine. "Hand me that, will you? Your story's driven me to drink."

Plates heaped high with fish and meat arrived a moment later. Most of the crew had adopted the tradition of ordering everything to share. Nel laughed to herself. It helped them try everything, but also provided a full stomach for the drinking later.

She ushered a piece of empanada onto her plate and dug in. Acrid flavor exploded in her mouth and she fought the urge to gag.

"Fuck, Nel, you okay?" Chad's hand hovered at her elbow.

She spat the mouthful into her napkin. "Yeah, just tastes like ass." An oily black knot nestled among the beef and peppers. She teased it out with her fork. "It's cloth or something." She spread it out and her stomach writhed further into a knot. A dead, mangled mouse sat in the center covered in a mixture of clotted blood and sauce.

"Must have fallen in when they were cooking," George hypothesized. "I used to work in kitchens and man, food isn't as clean as we think."

"Not now, George." Mikey's voice sharpened uncharacteristically. "What is it, Nel?"

"Bad publicity and some vandalism I can deal with, though it never makes me happy. I feel like I have to watch my back every second." She shoved back from her seat fast enough to knock it over. "I'm sorry guys, we're leaving. Now."

Emilio caught it before it clattered to the ground. He frowned. "Bently, my dear, what happened?"

"One of your fucking cooks is trying to kill me is what." She growled the words through her teeth as discreetly as possible.

His lips thinned in displeasure, dark eyes meeting hers for a moment before he jerked his head at her seat. "Stay. I'll make you something fresh myself."

She faltered, glancing at her crew sidelong. *If it was just me, it'd be one thing, but they're roping my students into this.* This was as much an attack on Emilio as on her diggers. "I can't Emilio, but thank you. Some other time."

The students had gathered their things. Nel watched as they filed out the door before following. The walk to the house was silent. The door banged shut behind them and Nel cleared her throat. "Hey, guys, one sec." The students paused, some halfway up the stairs. Annie looked like she was about to vomit. "I'm really sorry that happened. I know half the time I'm this pissed off stranger who grades your papers, but I do care and I want you to be safe here and have a good time. If you guys get hungry later come find me, okay?"

Sally offered a weak smile. "Thanks, Dr. Bently. I doubt any of us are in the mood for food, though. Have a good night."

Nel watched them retreat up the stairs. When the last door closed, she glanced over at Mikey. "You're quiet."

"You're scared." Mikey fished three beers from the fridge, popping the top on hers before handing it to her. "I haven't seen you scared in a long while. Angry, sure, but scared?"

She glanced at Chad, who watched them from the doorway. "It wasn't random trash that fell in a meal." She pulled out the cloth that had wrapped the mouse and spread it on the counter. The center was stitched with Los Pobladores' logo. "I'm worried. I can't believe I'm saying this, but I'd rather vandalism. They're involving the students and I'm done with that." She rubbed a hand over her face. "I'm ready to go to the cops."

Mikey pulled her into a tight hug. "Let's see how the next week goes. We can talk to the police then, okay?"

Nel nodded, but her stomach was still churning. No matter how many times she rinsed her mouth with beer, her tongue tasted only motor oil and rotten flesh.

Nel absently pulled up Los Pobladores' site again. She wasn't tired. It was torture, reopening a wound a hundred times just to see if it hurt less. She flicked through the pictures of their protests, half expecting to see her dig. *They wouldn't put that up. They know that's a low blow and would only make them look bad.* The computer collided with the wall when she shoved it away from her. Her heart raced in her chest as she stared at the most recent photo.

It was dimly lit and in selfie style, though the other person had been cropped out.

The caption was just as bad: "Bently promises that her destruction of our land and heritage is only a search for where humans can go, not out of respect or love of our culture and people." Leering up at her from the computer screen was Nel's own plastic-fake smile.

TEN

Nel swung into the driver's seat of the Jeep. The clatter of screen doors and field boots on the stairs heralded Mikey's approach. Each season they gave the crew a long weekend and took a Friday drive through the wilderness, looking for raw material. Usually they could pinpoint either a trade route or an actual source. Nel was bargaining some of her questions might have answers by the afternoon.

"Why do you get to drive?" Mikey's eyes were tired and bloodshot. He gripped his French press travel mug like a lifeline.

"Because you look like death. You drive back. You get water?"

"Yep."

"Field pack."

"Yep."

"Sunscreen?"

"Ugh." He tottered back inside only to reappear a minute later with sunscreen and his wallet. "K. Ready."

She pulled out onto the road, swaying easily with the lurching car. There was something primal about a bumpy road. Maybe it was her roots in the back-woods or that every site had class 6 roads, but they spoke to her soul.

"North or south?"

"North. Scant shit in the south. Plus, we can stop for lunch on the way."

"Gah, only if you pay."

He waved his wallet. "That's what rich backers are for. Can't expect us to find any rocks at all without good food."

Nel made a show of peering along the boulder-studded roadside. "Nope. No rocks here." She drove with one hand, fumbling with the Jeep's sound system. "Alright, since I'm driving, I choose the music."

Mikey groaned and slumped into the seat. "I was hoping to nap."

"Bullshit, you're on lookout."

Nel grinned wolfishly and slid an old cassette into the slot. "No better way to wake up than to Jay Z's melodic philosophies."

Mikey sighed and gazed dismally out the window. Nel snorted and grooved in the seat, pounding one hand on the wheel. She would be putting up as much of a fight when it was his turn. No one should listen to that much gospel. Ever.

She interrupted rapping about having 99 problems, "Alright, we're looking for that pink rock." She tugged a map of Chile's geography from her pack in the back seat. "See if you can get any ideas. I'm going down Route 1."

Mikey spread the map out on his lap. "Right. Rocks."

Nel bumped onto a side road. They'd never be able to see anything from the highway. She turned north and jerked the shifter into fourth.

By eleven, they'd crossed forty miles and had seen every kind of rock except pink. "You ready to break for lunch?"

"If it means I don't have to hear Gorillaz one more time, I'll say anything."

"Careful, you might regret that." She grinned and spun into a pull off. "You take over, I'll figure out what's closest." She slid the GPS from its case and climbed up onto the roll cage. "I swear our site is bugged, Mikey. This thing works fine everywhere else."

"Woooo, maybe it's aliens."

"Shut up, Mulder." Nel balanced on the steel bars, waving the GPS in the air. "Access code to me!" After a few moments, the device beeped into life. Nel tapped away at the screen, looking for any nearby restaurants. "La Merluza is a good 40 minutes away. There's a joint down Route 1 just outside of El Hueso and then a hole-in-the-wall a bit further down the road. Never heard of it."

"Hole-in-the-wall sounds good. Close?"

"Yeah, but you know the roads." Often it took an hour to go four miles. Mikey finally found the tape he wanted and popped it into the radio. "Ready when you are."

Nel hopped down and showed him the GPS. "Didn't even know there was a turnoff up there."

"Probably newer." He backed carefully out of the turn off and trundled onto the road again. His grin turned sly as he cranked the volume.

Nel kept her mouth tightly shut. Why someone who staunchly disbelieved in God loved southern gospel, she would never understand. "Turn left up here."

Mikey slowed, blinker invisible in the bright sun. The Jeep lurched and rattled down the slope. The empty road was old, the pavement closer to gravel. It was cut into the bedrock and Nel rose in her seat.

"Where did those boulders come from?"

"Honestly, it looks like the stuff from Alaska."

"Yeah, they probably just carried it the whole way. For generations."

Mikey rolled his eyes at her sarcasm. "People have done far stranger things."

"Yes, your music is a fine example of that." They rounded a bend and her eyes widened. "Shit."

Mikey slowed the car to a stop and cut the music. "I guess we found our answer."

"Holy fuck."

"Right? You bring the camera?"

Nel couldn't look away, and it took her three tries to hold the camera right-way-up. Just off the roadside to the left was a wall of familiar red stone.

A gorge burrowed into the cliff face, becoming a winding tunnel. Rusty-black veined the stone. The road curved past the tunnel, two hundred meters of steep embankment between the edge of the road and the rock face. "Wanna check it out?"

Mikey grinned. "Duh." He slid the Jeep onto the side of the road. Loaded down with packs, water, and the camera, they jogged across the road. "I think we'll have to just slide down on our asses."

Nel's whoop interrupted him as she swung over the guardrail and boot-skated down the gravel slope. Chile's landscape was a study in opposites— the lush forests and the Atacama. This was one of the green pockets. A river wound through the bottom of the canyon, an emerald snake in a desert of pink rock. A dozen flowers sweetened the air, and the muttering of the water drowned out the sound of the wind off the road far above. She edged into the canyon, running her hands along the wall. "Seriously, this is beautiful."

Mikey slid to a halt behind her. "How have we never heard about this?"

"It's off a back road. Locals probably know all about it, but it's not like this is a tourist destination. Probably wasn't even visible from the road until last year's quake." Nel followed the river deeper. It wasn't strictly a tunnel; gaps in the stone roof above shed dim, filtered pink light onto the clear water.

"When I die, Nel, this is where I want my ashes."

"Me too, dude." Nel stopped. "Oh, fuck, Mikey, look up."

The waving walls of stone were decorated with faded black hand-prints and other prints in relief. Nel pulled herself onto a shelf to get a better look. Further up were other prints, distorted and elongated.

"Charcoal?"

"No, too glittery. Looks like that black stuff layered on top of Strata III. How far are we from the site?"

"I left the GPS in the car. I don't suppose the camera can get any sort of reading under all this."

"Doubt it." Nel's gaze followed the river as it curved south and dove into a dark tunnel, winding deeper in the ground. "How much you want to bet this is the same river?"

"More than either of us make in a year."

"You think we could get funding for this?" She moved along the shelf and climbed higher. "Shit, there's art up here."

She heard Mikey scramble back to try and get a look. "Can't see it from here."

"Hold on, I'm taking a picture. It's on the ceiling up here. Can't really tell what it is. Looks like just designs." The shutter click echoed through the canyon a few times then she climbed down. "I'll grab a few shots further in, then let's head to lunch. I want to get back and see if I can find this online."

"I'm gonna grab some coordinates from the roadside. Holler if you need anything."

Nel followed the river bank for a few more feet, field book in hand as she sketched the river, the walls, anything she could fit on the pages.

"Nel!"

"Hold on." She copied the designs and took another few shots with her camera phone before finally turning back.

Mikey's shouting was faint all the way down the embankment, but when she emerged from the tunnel his words were suddenly clear.

"Nel, get your ass back up here!" His tone was unusually tense.

She jogged up, skittering and catching herself twice before she reached the guardrails. Her heart sank. Mikey stood by the Jeep, hands in the air.

Emilio and two men she recognized by face surrounded their car, gun's trained on Mikey's pissed expression. Their Land Rover was studded with political stickers and hand-painted designs.

"Oh fuck."

"Bently, drop the bag."

"Can I get out of the road, Emilio?" When he nodded curtly, she crossed over and dropped her field pack at their feet. She leaned against the Jeep by Mikey, but refused to raise her hands. "Since when do you guys carry guns?"

"Since you refuse to listen." The younger of the two spat."

She narrowed her eyes. "You were watching us the first day we broke ground."

"Gringo. Can't tell us apart."

"Don't be an ass, Bas. You were there." Emilio rolled his eyes and upended their packs. "Search the car if you're too bored." Nel winced. Emilio chucked the rock samples over the rail, wiped the camera card, and ripped out the most recent pages of her field book. "You realize every time you warn us, it just tells us we're closer? You think you're discouraging? I think you're leaving bread crumbs."

"Nel." Mikey's warning shut her up, but didn't wipe the cocky contempt from her face. Within fifteen minutes everything they had collected was destroyed.

"Bently, you need to get in that car, turn around, and not look back. You come here again and I'll be waiting."

"Mikey, wanna grab a bite?"

"Sounds good. I'm in the mood for something spicy." He climbed into the driver seat and fiddled with the radio while she stalked around the car. She spit at Emilio's boots before slamming the door shut.

"See you around, Asshole."

Nel jabbed the radio and cranked the volume, not caring that it was a juvenile display. Their tires spun as Rage Against the Machine blasted over the desolate road.

They pulled out, spraying the three men with gravel and exhaust. As soon as they were out of ear-shot, Mikey turned the music down. "What the fuck! We lost everything. And if you say you're going back, I'll personally throw you in the China Trench and let you rot."

"Yeah, they got most of it, but they didn't search us." She pulled her cell out. "The pics aren't pretty, but they're better than nothing."

ELEVEN

The site maps and aerials had been weighted to Nel's desk for so long that they lay flat on their own. Her hand cramped around the red pencil she used to mark places that had been recorded by the GIS. "This is fucked up." Without looking from the map, she pounded on the wall between her and Mikey's rooms. "Oi, Dirt-brain, check this out."

He emerged a moment later, blinking sleep from his bloodshot eyes. "Dude, you know I nap at this time."

She glanced at her clock. 4:00. "Sorry, thought it was still 3:00, my bad. Look at this, though." She pointed to the site map. "What do you see?"

"I see Relano VII, the site you worked your ass off to get permits for." When her scowl deepened, he turned back. "Right. Sorry."

She watched his fingers trace the red marks. He paused, turned the map upside down, and looked again.

"Looks like a sluice way or something."

"Yeah, but look at the grade. Not the surface one, I mean the one in Strata II."

"What grade?"

"Exactly. That's perfectly flat. Mikey. Not natural, that's for sure."

"I didn't know the paleos did landscaping. Not on this scale at least."

"They don't. Their decedents may have carved giant stones into people, sure, but this is older. We haven't found a single piece of red ocher. Some in the site proper, but nothing out there so it's not ceremonial."

"This is weird. You get any carbon?"

"Yeah, mixed with the dark stuff in the top few centimeters of Strata III."

"Uniform across, right?"

"Uniform. Got samples, sent them to the lab in Santiago to see what the dates and composition data says. Maybe we'll find out what happened to these people. There's certainly no evidence for a volcano." Nel perched on the edge of her desk, staring at the maps. She had memorized them. She could draw it in her sleep.

Mikey sank onto her bed, staring out the window. "Still doesn't answer one thing, though."

"What's that?"

"Why the damned Flounders are so pissed that we found it."

Nel sidled along the wall. Goosebumps peppered her skin and she swallowed hard. *Mikey would die if he saw me right now.* Forethought had never been her specialty. Still, if Los Pobladores were going to fight dirty, fuck it, so would she. When they first vandalized her site two years ago, she had gone to the local police, angry and full of foreigner's entitlement. She knew better now. This was their world, a world she visited and loved and studied. It was a feral cat that crawled into her, made a home in a corner of her soul, but would never be hers.

She paused at the corner, watching the bustle of the restaurant ahead. The bright glow against the cool darkness of night was twisted now. The welcoming yellow was tainted with cowardice. *I'm not much better.* She didn't know what she was looking for. She didn't know what she would find. She only knew she couldn't sit, idle, when Los Pobladores practiced the archaeological equivalent of guerilla warfare.

Gravel ground under her boots and she stilled. The buildings reached back from the street, different parts of lives layered before one another until they spilled on to the road. Behind the restaurant was the family house, spread wide for generations, and beyond that a tidy, lush garden, complete with a shed.

Except it wasn't a garden shed. Built back into the encroaching hills, its windows were blackened. A collection of wind chimes and tattered flags hung along the roofline, all a very obvious red. She entertained the idea of bursting in with a sharpened trowel and snarling for them to leave her alone. She would discover they had actually been doing something rather more illegal than fucking up her site, and thusly she would be made a local hero. She grinned at her fantasy. *I'm no Lara Croft.*

She crept along the fence and up to the shed. The overgrown garden provided cover from the rear of the house, but if anyone watched from the windows above, she would be caught in moments. Rough palm rasped against rough wood and the door opened.

The shed was just a shed, really. The air was dim and filled with dust and dirt. The smell of age and sand interspersed with something acrid, like spilled oil. Her boots scuffed against dried planks swept clean, bumping into a worktable.

A stack of papers rustled and she flipped her phone open for light. There were a dozen photos of her site, her crew, the Vicuña y Las Rosas, and the crown jewel image of her with Emilio. They were printed on cheap paper, the edges dulled and wilted from sweaty hands. There was a crew shot she had taken just days ago and e-mailed to Martos and their benefactors. The fact that Los Pobladores had access to her email, whether via hacking or infiltration, didn't even make her angry. It was a violation, sure, but seeing her work torn apart was a violation violent enough to make most others fade.

She straightened, holding her phone steady with both hands before snapping a photo of the arrayed images. She'd be stupid to go to the police, what with her trespassing, but she needed proof that this wasn't another figment of her heat-addled brain. *They might just be ghosts to the locals, they might be boogeymen to our benefactor, but they're fucking real to me.*

She glanced around, taking stock of the room once more. There was little else to see. A battered lock-box could have held trash or treasure. Gardening tools hung on the wall. Her gaze stuttered to a halt at the narrow door leading further back into the hill. It was old, older than the shed, maybe, and fastened at the top and middle with mismatched padlocks.

That's a door for secrets. Nel had little interest in becoming a felon in a foreign country, but the explorer in her itched to break the lock from the weathered wood and find out what, exactly, the Founders wanted from her. Her fingers traced the grain of the old wood, the glint of the new locks. *Old secrets, new protectors.* She sighed and pulled herself away. The journey back to the house took far longer than her creeping walk had, like her body moved through honey, pulled back to the space her thoughts still rested. There was something that niggled at the back of her mind, an idea planted by the secrecy of her benefactors, the anger of the founders. She was certain the answer lay behind an old door and new locks.

TWELVE

"Lunch!" Mikey's shout boomed across the site, followed by the clatter of shovels, trowels, and buckets hitting the ground. Nel finished mapping another rock before meandering back to the shade of the pop-up. She fumbled around the cooler, eyes still fixed on the map. Finally, she found a bottle and settled against one of the poles. The crew was quiet, excited chewing punctuated with the buzz of insects and tinny music played through a smart phone.

Nel took a heavy swig off her water bottle. Bitter juniper burst across her tongue and she gagged, whirling to spew the mouthful onto the ground behind her. "Fuck!" She peered closer at the cap of the bottle. She had scrawled a "G" onto the plastic with a permanent marker, but the ice had turned black into faint grey. She glanced up to see the crew staring at her, a mixture of concern and friendly contempt on their faces.

She grimaced. "That is the last damn time I'm reusing water bottles for gin. Three times now I've brought alcohol into the field."

"Rookie mistake, Dr. Bently!" George's banter broke the eager silence of eating.

Mikey leaned forward. "What's everyone brought today?"

Some had brought left overs, others a simple sandwich. *And some make rookie mistakes and bring fucking alcohol into the field instead of water.* Nel took Mikey's proffered bottle and swished the taste from her mouth.

Food was a constant subject. Morning topics would be the best lunches everyone had ever had. Lunch-time was for sharing and discussing supper. The afternoon's food discussion would go between serious propositions for meals and blatant food-porn. Nel listened to the options for a few minutes while she wolfed down her salad.

"I want to try that little place on the corner again," Annie said. "I saw something on their menu the other night but I'd already ordered."

"We've been there twice this week. We could go next week," Sally suggested.

"Next week is for El Cóndor and that'll take half our per diem. Besides, they've got so much stuff, it's not really like you'll have to get the same thing."

Nel cleared her throat. "I don't suppose anyone would be interested in having a crew cook-out tonight. There's a butcher in town that has great cuts and I make a mean jalapeno glazed chicken. We could all pitch in and make our best potluck stuff. I've got some spices in the kitchen for people to use."

Her suggestion was met with groans of happiness and she grinned into her lunch. Mikey's eyes narrowed on her with mock anger. Nel stuck her tongue out in response. She might not be the social crack that Mikey was, but she knew how to romance hungry diggers.

"Oi, got something for you to see." Chad leaned on one leg of the pop-up tent.

Nel glanced up absently from organizing the buckets of artifacts and soil samples. "You find something?"

"No, still no artifacts, but we're done profiling that unit and have the profiles from all the STPs lined up too. It's interesting."

Nel tossed a last bag into a bucket and dusted her hands off. "Have you taken anything for analysis yet?"

"No, thought you might have specifics about that."

Nel followed him across the site to the unit he and Annie had dug on the ridge. It was 1m square and close to 80 cm deep. The soils were the usual three layers, save for the black band cutting through the B stratum. Nel crouched down and drew her trowel. The 3cm lens was compact, but composed of fine grains. She didn't know what it was, but Mikey's words rang in her ears. "Chad, call the rest of the crew over. We should talk about this as a group."

When the others crowded around, Nel gestured to the unit. "What do you think, Annie?"

"Me?" Annie knelt carefully next to Nel. "I'm not sure it's a stain—"

"Be confident." Nel glanced over her shoulder. "If you truly think something, own it. Worst case, you'll be wrong and learn something."

Annie laughed softly. "I don't think it's a stain. The consistency is different from that above and below it. It's like an alluvial deposit, but I'm not sure—but this isn't the proper area for a flood. We're too high and there's a stream below that would be a more probable path for a flood. There's also almost no bioturbation in this area, so I doubt a rodent or roots carried this down from the surface. Besides it's too uniform for that to be the actual source."

Nel sat back, a small chunk of the dark soil on her trowel. "Good. I agree." She dumped the chunk into George's hand. "Pass this around, feel it with your fingers, smell it—don't eat it please, Henri—really look at it. Does it remind you of something you've seen before on another dig? Maybe you've seen something similar somewhere else, unrelated to archaeology."

The dirt was passed around, most of the diggers examining it with clueless earnestness. Kat tilted her head at it thoughtfully "This looks like metal, you know?"

Nel glanced up. "What do you mean?"

"My dad has this grinder in his work shop, for metal and sharpening stuff, you know? This pile of metal filings collects under it and it looks like this."

Nel clenched her jaw. Kat was observant, but her speech patterns grated against every nerve Nel had left. "Good, thanks." She rose with a sigh. "Alright, everyone back to work." She turned to Annie. "Annie, I want you to take a sample of this. You won't want to contaminate it in anyway. They probably won't do much protein analysis on it, but just to be safe we'll be sterile." She handed Annie a packet of sterile gloves and two plastic bags. "Wash your trowel with distilled water, over there, and wipe it down. Then scrape down very carefully until you have enough to fill that bag. We'll record the location of your sample and send it out tomorrow morning."

Nel plopped down with a sigh on one of the big rocks. The stone on metal grinders was silicate in nature, but most of the dust was from the metal itself. What were metal filings doing in the middle of intact geological strata?

THIRTEEN

The heat made Nel's head pound and her heart flutter. She kicked the shovel into the ground, heaving another scoop of dirt into the waiting screen. She paired the crew off for such things, but preferred to work alone. There were only three more test pits left in between the stone lines. *I want these done by the end of the day.* Henri probably had another level, at least, before he came down onto the C horizon, but there had been precious little in the unit, save for the beautiful point. Still, one unbroken diagnostic was enough in Nel's book.

She dropped the shovel in the pit and stepped over the hole to raise the screen. The sound of dry, rocky earth against 1/8 inch metal mesh drowned out everything except Nel's pounding heart and the hot breath billowing in her lungs. She paused, rough hands brushing through the pile of pebbles and potential flakes. *Nothing.* She flicked the examined rocks onto the back dirt pile and was about to lift the shovel again when Mikey's whistle shot up the hill.

She shielded her eyes. He waved her over to Henri's unit. His mouth was thin and his brow furrowed. *Fuck, what now? This site is a mess as it is.* She grabbed her field book and jogged down the slope. "What's up?"

Mikey jerked his chin at the unit. Henri crouched on the edge, eyes wide and trowel pointing at the bottom of the level. "Dr. Bently, I think we've got something big."

The soil was not the uniform brown that the B horizon should have been. Instead a dark stain covered one full corner and disappeared into the wall. Nel leaned down, scraping some of the dirt into her hand. She ground it between her fingers, tilting her palm so the light caught on the tiny grains of silt and sand. It was dark and slick, as if someone had spilled cooking oil. She sat back on her heels. Preservation of bodies only happened under the most ideal circumstances. Usually, all that was left were bone fragments and residual grease from ancient decomposition.

"Yeah, this is big alright." She glanced up at Henri. "I'm putting Chad with you—not because you're doing poorly, but because he has more experience with this. You're going to go down by 5cm levels now, and stop at anything unusual. Bone will be like dry tan clay. At each level, please map in the staining and anything you find."

"This is a burial, isn't it?"

"It's something, that's for sure. Can't say if it's human or not, but my money's on yes, especially with that point above it. Could be that was a grave good." She grinned. "You just put this site on the map."

The heavy envelope survived only until Nel's door latched behind her. She tore it across the end and tugged the tri-folded composition results from safety. She peered at them, lips thinning. Spectroscopy results were hard to understand on the best of days. "Complex hydrocarbons? Magnetized metal dust?" None of the molecules looked familiar. She wasn't a chemist, but she could recognize the spectrometer's readouts depicting charcoal, various rocks and metals. "Ugh, this is a mess!" She grabbed her cell and dialed the lab. "Could I have Dr. Danilo Salinas. This is Dr. Bentley." She flipped through the other pages, finding similar results.

The line clicked. "Salinas's Taco Stand."

Nel wasn't in the mood for his usual jokes. "Just got the results. What the hell am I looking at?"

"Lemme pull up the data so I can walk you through it. Alright, got it. The control samples you sent are the usual—actually looks like a remarkably clean site. Came back with your local dirt make-up for that strata—silica, trace clays. The kicker was the black stuff. It's metal, almost completely, and the composition is from all over. We isolated it and ran some other fun tests—it's extremely light, but magnetized somehow. The black stuff is metallic, and it's got some sort of petroleum residue."

Nel stared at the report, phone held between her ear and shoulder. "This isn't fucking right."

"Sorry, Nel. We ran it three times. Looks like you got a contaminated site. We're running the dates and we'll get them to you as soon as possible, but at this point it's just a formality. I very much doubt the paleos had rocket fuel."

She hung up without saying good-bye. Danilo took a bit too much enjoyment from her difficulties. *He could join Los Pobladores and I probably wouldn't notice a difference.*

FOURTEEN

Two days of careful excavation sat mapped on the table, along with several dozen little bags. She brushed a hand over the fragment of femur. *Fifteen thousand years and this is all that's left of a living, breathing person. Someone with hopes and dreams, someone who had friends, family.*

"You alright, Nel?" Chad leaned on the tent leg.

"Humbled, is all." The bones were anatomically modern human, enough left to show naturally decaying edges. *And a few wounds that never healed.* She pointed to the map that had each bone located. "Some of these look like they might be perimortem."

"Think they met an untimely end?"

"Maybe. They were buried, that's for sure. I'm curious to see what that point brings back—if it was unused it might have been a grave good."

"When will the data come back?"

"Should be waiting for me when we get back. Danilo promised to push it through after ruining my day on Tuesday." She collected the bags and tucked them carefully into her pack with the maps.

Chad snorted and helped her pack away the rest of the day's finds. "That guy has too much fun messing up our days. I assume you're going to expand the unit on all sides?"

"Yeah, on Monday. I'm just glad we got all this out before the weekend. I'd hate to leave something so precious for Los Pobladores to fuck with." She clipped the tool box closed and hoisted it onto her shoulder with her pack. "Mikey, you coming?"

He was still bent over the total station, glasses perched like a mayfly on his nose. "I want to get this thing re-calibrated. I'll hike down in a few."

"K. I got something to show you, though, so come see me when you get back."

He waved absently, showing he'd heard, fingers already twirling the various pegs on the yellow case. Nel shoved the Jeep into first and rumbled down the road. Between weird residue and malfunctioning equipment, her site was setting a record for strange.

Nel leaned back in the chair. It creaked softly in the warm night. The screen door banged as the students traipsed out for their nightly drinking.

"Remember that?" Chad eased himself into the chair beside her.

"I do. Now I'm too lazy to bother getting spiffy. I'll settle for a dirty-beer and a quiet porch."

He nodded and tipped back his gin and tonic. "Do you ever miss it?"

"Hell no. At least, I don't miss the bar scene. I could use a little fun though."

"CRM is good for that. I like the crew mentality. Everyone cooks and drinks together then passes out at 9:00."

Nel laughed. "I do miss the food. Damn, you remember Carl's Bar-B-Q?"

"Fucking heaven. One of my favorite humans."

They were silent for several moments, listening to the buzz of insects and street lights. Nel tilted her head back, eyes closed. "Damn, today just took it out of me." A frown shadowed her face, but she didn't open her eyes. "Mikey come home yet?"

"No. No surprise, though. He was pissed at the total station. He tried to recalibrate it twice today."

Nel groaned. "That thing sucks. Sometimes I miss just measuring off the datum."

"It's a great tool, but technology is rough." He drained his drink.

After a moment Nel stood and stretched. "I'm going to go shower and maybe nap."

"What're you having for dinner?"

Nel shrugged. "No idea. It's almost too hot to eat. I'll knock if I'm headed out. When you see Mikey, send him my way."

Nel stared at the open email. The protein analysis glared up at her from the screen. She had seen tools with caribou, rodent, even bear. She'd never expected the tool to be positive for human proteins.

She quickly forwarded the data to Mikey and Martos before flicking open her phone. Her brows snapped together when her call went straight to Mikey's voicemail. "Hey, Mikey, it's me. Just wondering where you got to. Protein analysis is back, got something interesting you need to see. Come find me when you're back."

She hung up then dialed Martos. He was often in the office late.

"Dr. Javier Martos."

"Hey, it's Bently."

"Ah, how're things going?"

"Alright. Had some local color, but nothing we couldn't handle." She hesitated. She hadn't mentioned the encounter with Los Pobladores on the highway yet and had a bad feeling it would get her funding revoked. "Got some news for you. We got a body."

"In situ? How intact? Is it a burial?"

Nel laughed. "I've sent you all the details. Looks like it's a burial and fairly intact. Close to a hundred bones. Got them all mapped in now. I'm thinking it wasn't a natural death, though."

"Broken bones?"

"There's some perimortem damage, yeah, but more than that. We found a point just above it, which was unusual for grave goods. I got the analysis back and It's positive for human protein, Martos."

"What?"

"Yep. Looks like we've got us a murder weapon."

FIFTEEN

Nel woke with a start. The hammering was not in her head, but on the door downstairs. She knew that knock—someone official. "Son of a whore, I don't want to deal with vandals today." If Los Pobladores did something bad enough to get the attention of the cops, they were in for trouble. "Probably trashed the Jeep again." She tugged on her dig clothes from the day before and hurried downstairs. Being Saturday morning, everyone else was thankfully still in bed. Whatever new mess she had to handle was better done in private.

The officer downstairs was one she recognized from the year before when she filed for her local permits. The heavy-set man behind him was wearing the official uniform of the Policia de Investigaciones.

She stopped on the stairs. "Fuck, Munoz, what now? I've told you a thousand times, there's no use pressing charges. You agreed with me about it last time."

The officer's grim lines deepened. "Nel, please."

"Dr. Nel Bently?" The other man stepped forward.

"Yeah?" She crossed her arms. As a rule, she disliked anything bigger than the local governments.

"You got a digger named Servais?"

"He's my site manager, yeah. I haven't seen him this morning, but I can go get him. What's up?" A door opened and shut above her. A moment later Chad appeared a step behind her. Nel flashed him a weak smile.

"I'm sorry to be the one to tell you this, Dr. Bently, but Dr. Servais is dead."

The still air roared in Nel's ears. The stairs pitched under her feet and suddenly she was sitting and Chad's hands were on her shoulders. "I'm sorry?"

Munoz pressed a glass of water into her hand. "Some local boys found his body off the main road a few miles out of town. Looks like homicide."

Nel abruptly remembered why she disliked big-city cops. The further they were from actual people the further they were from reality. Words like "homicide" and "investigation" meant nothing when your best friend was dead.

SIXTEEN

Nel stared out the window. The air was warm, the sun high, and the sky clear. She suspected if it were any other day, it would have been called beautiful. The fact remained, however, that it was the day after her best friend died. Such a day could never be called beautiful. Martos had once said she and Mikey were a perfect pair, one the energetic version of the other—driven and patient, passionate and caring.

Martos had been right in his descriptors, but he had been wrong in one thing. She wasn't driven. She wasn't passionate. She was angry. It wasn't the hot, sudden anger of adolescence, or the tired trope of the lesbian, angry at being misunderstood. It was the slow, steady heat of the earth's core. It drove her studies and fueled her curiosity. Mikey's death punched a hole through the thick shell she carefully curated to contain her rage. It spewed, unchecked and aimless into every thought and action. Mugs and plates and the case for the total station's back-up battery dotted the floor, victims of her fury.

There were a thousand things she had to do, she supposed. A thousand things that would burn the minute she touched them. So, instead, she sat.

It took three attempts before she realized the pounding was not the pulsing of her anger, but Chad's knocking. She cleared her throat. "What."

His words were shapeless humming through the wood, and when she didn't answer, he cracked the door and tried again. "We need to talk to the crew. I'd do it, but they know you better. Or, at least, it's your job and not mine."

She heard the door open farther and the sigh of the bed as he sat. "Please, Nel. This sucks, but they don't know what's going on and they're scared. The cops want to talk to you and Martos called and said you weren't picking up."

She cleared her throat again. It was tight and her eyes stung. *I must have caught a cold.* "We'll have to send them home. If the cops let them."

"Yeah. I know." She surged from her chair. "I'll text them to be home for lunch." Her fingers stilled their tapping across her phone's keyboard. Chad still waited in the doorway. "What?"

"They've shut down the dig. Pulled your permits for auditing."

Nel froze by her desk. It was the obvious outcome. She had known the moment Munoz said "homicide" their work would stop. Hearing it in Chad's soft, careful words, a voice more disposed to joking and beauty, made the reality sharp. "I'll call the precinct, ask when the kids can leave, then I'll talk to them."

A terse call to the police and several swigs of cold coffee later, Nel was closer to being prepared than before. She flipped open her phone and sent a mass text:

> *Meet me in the kitchen in an hour. Please don't be late. Mandatory.*

Chad gathered the chairs and stools into some semblance of seating. Nel stood behind the counter, staring into the mug of coffee before her when they arrived. She couldn't bring herself to look up until the conversation had died and the shuffling of sandals and seats had ceased. "Thank you for being prompt. This hasn't been a good weekend. I have some bad news and some worse news. I appreciate if you save questions until I have finished." *I won't get through this with interruptions*. She cleared her throat, making sure her gaze moved from one student to the next, not really seeing them.

"The volunteer student program at the site is terminated indefinitely. Tomorrow each of you will need to go down to the local police department. I will be driving us all. None of you are in trouble, but you will need to answer some questions about

Friday as well as other things, I imagine. Please be honest. They don't care if you've been drinking, if you've hooked up with the local boys or girls. You will all leave for home by the end of the week. I'll help arrange your tickets and cover the cost of any issues. I will call your families this evening to explain things to them myself and answer any questions, but I suggest you call them first. They'd like to hear that you're safe from your mouths."

Her gaze fell to the counter top. "I thought I'd start with the bad news, to ease you into the worse. Friday night, Mikey stayed behind at the site to fix the calibration on the total station. He never made it home. His body was found on the side of the road yesterday morning. I know many of you were closer to Mikey than you were to me, and I'm sorry that you've lost a valuable mentor. If you need to talk about it, Chad or I will gladly listen. If you would feel more comfortable, I can help you find someone on campus back home." Her voice echoed monotonously in her ears, drowning out all other sounds save for the roar of blood in her head. "Please meet me down here at 7:00 a.m. tomorrow morning. We'll get coffee before we arrive at the precinct. That'll be it."

No one moved for a moment, and Nel cursed inwardly. She didn't want to look at their bewildered faces. She wanted to be alone. Tentative steps approached and suddenly sunburnt arms wrapped around her shoulders.

"Dr. Bently, I'm so sorry."

Nel stiffened. She wasn't a hugger and embracing students was something they were strictly warned against, but she couldn't bring herself to push away. "Thanks, Annie."

She stepped back and gave them all an awkward nod before heading for the stairs. She wasn't ready for a wave of emotion and sympathy to break over her head. She wasn't ready for much of anything.

SEVENTEEN

Nel's phone blinked with three missed calls: two from Martos and a third from a number she didn't recognize. *There goes my funding.* She listened to Martos first. He clearly hadn't known when he called. With a sigh she dialed him back and waited. He picked up on the first ring.

"Nel?"

"Hey. Sorry, I was away from my phone."

"The police left a message on my work phone, but didn't tell me what was wrong, just to call them back. What happened? Did they screw up the site? Are you all safe?"

"The students are fine. Martos, they got Mikey."

"What happened? Is he out of the hospital?"

"The cops showed up this morning. Some kid found his body on the side of the road." The lack of reply hissed through the phone line. If it weren't for the sounds of a kitchen in the background, Nel would have thought he had hung up. "I don't know what to do, Martos." It was something she could admit only to him and Mikey.

"They'll suspend your permits, and I assume you can't come home due to the investigation."

"They already have."

"Have you spoken to the police?"

"Not really. I wasn't listening much to what they said. We're going to the station tomorrow. The students have to make statements. We all do. Chad's been a help. Thanks for sending him."

"It wasn't like I knew."

"None of us did."

"It's stupid to ask, but how are you holding up?"

"Everything is distant. I'm not really in this world right now."

"I'm sorry. I know you two were close."

"So were you."

"Even still. If there's anything I can do…. Do you want me to handle calling his family?"

"They know me—we've met several times. I think they'd appreciate it better coming from me. I don't know what to say, really. I've never been good about this stuff. I didn't think I was a griever."

"This is different. Listen, I'll handle the legal stuff, and feel free to conference me in when you talk to the police. Let me know when you've called his family too."

"I'll phone them in a few minutes." She fell silent, listening to his breathing through the line. "I guess I should go. I'm sorry. I'm sorry I'm not better at this. I'm sorry I didn't stop the dig sooner."

"You should be sorry for nothing, Nel. Don't go down that road. I'll talk to you tomorrow, if not sooner. Try and get some rest."

The phone call to Mikey's dad was the worst thing Nel had ever had to do. She had no explanations, no kind words or heroic actions to sooth the wound of losing a child. She could not say his death had been quick, but silence was better than the truth. Seeing someone cry was bad, but listening to a grown man weep over the phone, hearing every hiccup of pain in his voice, was far worse. She wanted to cry with him, knew it would ease the icy mass of lead in her chest. The tears just wouldn't come.

Nel perched on the rooftop. The cool evening air was balm against her cheeks. She hadn't been downstairs, been into his room since yesterday. The raucous night noise echoed up from the town, a tiny window into a world devoid of grief.

Chad's street shoes scuffed on the stucco. "Can I join you."

She nodded. Her throat was raw from screaming and shouting and weeping. Words weren't important enough.

"It sounds stupid to say I'm sorry. I liked Mikey, but he was something else to you. I can't think of what to say, other than too much, it seems."

She shrugged. Being alone was better, but she was so far removed from the world, that even in Chad's talkative company, she was isolated. "I talked to Martos." Her voice cracked into being, a gravely monotone response.

"Did he know?"

She shook her head once. "I had to tell Mikey's dad." She kicked absently at the chimney. "This is all my fault, Chad."

"Like fuck it is."

"I told Mikey at the beginning of the season, I was worried someone might get hurt. I should have told him to wait to calibrate the damn total station. I should have waited for him. I should have listened when Los Pobladores warned us two weeks ago."

"You couldn't have known it would go this far."

"They held us up on the side of the road. With a gun. I should have known."

"Nel, fight them. Fight this fucking mess. Don't destroy yourself."

"They want us at the station first thing tomorrow."

He looked away, clearly knowing better than to argue. "I'll drive you."

EIGHTEEN

Chad was a better driver than Nel expected, and the drive to the station was quick. Annie pulled into the parking lot a moment after. Nel returned the girl's faint smile and led the way into the building. She was briefly glad she had the forethought to bring something other than cargo pants and dig shirts. A good set of clothes gave her the illusion of armor.

Officer Munoz and the Policia from before stepped out of an interrogation room as Chad was being patted down at the entrance. Munoz offered a nod. "Dr. Bently, thanks for coming down. This is Inspector Reyes, from Antofagasta."

Nel shook both their hands and gestured to Chad. "This is Dr. Chad Calligaris. He's one of the other head diggers I have. Had." She shook the thought away and jerked her head at the line of students. "These are the students."

"Dr. Calligaris, I'm sure we'll want to speak with you too, but for the time being I'll talk to Dr.

Bently alone." Munoz rested a hand on her arm and ushered her down the hall. She followed him into a small, dim room equipped with a table and a few chairs. A coffee maker sputtered in the corner beside a trashcan overfull with cold, wet grounds and filters. She took the indicated seat, glancing up to note the camera in the corner and the heavy lock on the door.

"You're not under investigation, really, but we have to be thorough." Reyes perched on a corner of the table, eyes too curious for Nel's comfort.

"Of course." Nel swallowed hard. Their words were like a script, one she didn't like. "Anything I can do to help."

"The questions I have won't be easy, and I want you to know we're doing everything we can. Your understanding and patience during such a trying time is appreciated."

I haven't been patient yet. "I understand."

"Can you detail the last time you saw Dr. Servais?"

"Friday. We had a long day in the field. I was driving the crew back, but he said he'd stay behind to calibrate our total station—the survey machine that helps us map the location of finds and stuff. It was out of whack."

"Did you receive any phone calls? Anything?"

"Nothing until you came Saturday morning. I asked to talk to him when he got back, but I fell asleep early, so I didn't think anything of not seeing him that night."

"What was your relationship with Dr. Servais?" Reyes tilted his head. He lacked all of Munoz's warmth and kindness.

Nel laughed humorlessly. "Not whatever you're thinking. We're friends. Good ones. I've known him since undergrad. He's not exactly my type."

"Ah. Do you know if he was intimate with any of the crew? Any locals?"

"None of the crew. He had a girlfriend back home, but they broke up a few months before we came here. He met a woman at a bar recently, but it didn't sound like anything romantic. I think he would have told me if it was."

"Can you think of anyone who would have wanted to hurt him? Did he owe money? Have any gambling or drinking problems?" Reyes asked.

Nel just stared at him. She wished Munoz would jump in to defend Mikey. He had known them both for years. "You can't be serious."

The Investigator pinched the bridge of his nose. "Please humor me."

"Humor you? My best friend was found *dead* on the side of the damned fucking road, we both know exactly who did it, and you are asking me to *humor* you?"

Munoz held his hand up. "I'm sorry for your loss, Ms. Bentley, truly, I am. I can only guess what you're feeling and thinking. Please realize we want to solve this as much as you."

"This has Los Pobladores written all over it!"

"How? They've never been violent. They've only staged peaceful protests. There was no evidence on the body or along the roadside."

Nel looked down. The numbness that carried her through the night before in one piece trembled under the logic. *He's right. I know it was them. I know they threatened us, but they're not stupid.* "If I gave you names, stuff they touched and my own prints for comparison, do you think it would help?"

"They touched your belongings?"

Her eyes flicked back up to his, burning with tears and something hot and roiling in her chest. "They held us at gunpoint on the roadside a few weeks ago. Their names are Emilio Sepulveda and Bastian something. They should be easy to find— Emilio owns the place downtown." She slid her chair out. "I'll get you the equipment out of the car when we're done. Now, if you'd humor me, I'd like to see his body."

Reyes's face finally faltered. "I understand wanting to see him, to say goodbye. Unfortunately, we're still examining his body for evidence. We'll let you know as soon as you can see him. I think I have all the answers I need for now. I'll bring you out to your students."

Nel did not answer and followed him back up the hall.

NINETEEN

Nel held her beer against her shoulder, swaying in front of the jukebox. She had already been asked to change the song by two people. She hoped it was her nasty response that sent them packing, but she knew it was the bloodshot condition of her eyes. Later, when her thoughts were more ordered and had been drained of alcohol, she would be grateful to Jerod for not asking her to leave or turn the music off.

She snuffled into her sleeve. She wanted every one of Mikey's favorite songs to be tattooed on her mind. Her field boot thumped softly against the worn floor. It was made for dancing, made for drunken release and laughter. She supposed it was good for drunken rage too.

Her phone chuttered in her pocket and she flipped it open. One eye refused to focus on the tiny print of Chad's text.

Just dropped the kids off at the airport. I'm dealing with this end of the paperwork while I'm here. I'll be home tomorrow (Friday). Take care of yourself.

She did not respond. She popped another quarter into the machine. Her hips swayed again, without any real rhythm.

There was so much about Mikey that she never thought to ask. He was a perfect set of opposites. An atheist who loved gospel songs. A crass, dirty-minded romantic. She took it all as just "being Mikey." Now she wish she had asked. The screen door slammed shut as someone stepped into the smoky, dim interior. Every local knew that door spring was broken. The startled curse suggested this was no local. The clack of heels against the worn wood confirmed it. "Excuse me, I'm looking for the Vicuña y Las Rosas."

The woman's Spanish was impeccable, the kind of fluent one only developed by immersion. Nel screwed her eyes shut. She did not want to deal with reporters right now. She was liable to swear and make an ass of herself. *Mikey always handled the PR.*

The bartender, Jerod, cleared his throat. "They're all booked out, but there's an inn on the other side of town."

The woman's briefcase thumped onto one of the barstools. "I'm looking for a woman staying there, actually. Annelise Bently. I'm from Santiago."

"You're sure not from around here. It's down the road a ways. Turn left at the red three-story." There was a pregnant pause as he waited to see if she left. "Not sure if she's in. If I see her, who should I say was asking?"

"You think you're likely to see her in a bar at ten in the morning?" When Jerod refused to answer, the woman cleared her throat. "I'm Lin Nalawangsa from the Institute for the Development of Humanity."

"What did you just say?" Nel turned slowly, but the floor still bucked under her boots. She caught herself on the edge of a booth.

The woman's perfect black brows shot up. She wore a navy pantsuit right out of a '90s police procedural. "Excuse me?"

"Who'd you say you were?"

"It's not important." She pointedly turned back to Jerod. "Thank you, sir."

Nel managed to organize two full sentences by the time the woman reached the door. "I'm Nel. Los Cerros Esperando VII is mine."

Lin's brows shot even higher. She glanced at Jerod. "I see." She slid onto a bar stool.

Nel stumbled over and sat one stool away. "Give me something with balls, Jerod. I think one of us will need them." She turned sideways and stared at Lin. Her skin was the soft gold that Nel's only dreamed about. She was too polished for Nel's tastes, but the kind of porceline-pretty that suited a model. Her features spoke of Southeast Asian heritage, but her accent was odd. "Why are you here? We got shut down. No need for you to get your hands dirty. Could have pulled our funding with a nice long 'fuck-you' on company letterhead."

"Ms. Bently I didn't come to pull your funding."

"First of all, don't call me 'Ms.' Second of all, if you ever say Annelise I'll smash this glass over your head. Third of all, you'll talk plainly, or I'm walking out." She considered her drink for a moment. "I'd make you walk out. I'm not done drinking yet."

"Right. Nel. We heard about the accident and I came to help. We're not pulling funding. I'm filing paperwork to reopen your site."

Nel knocked back half her drink. It was one of Jerod's weird concoctions with extra coconut milk. It was Mikey's favorite. She glanced up at the bartender through a narrow tunnel of clarity. "Thanks, Jer. This is really good."

"Nel." Lin's voice was low, but pointed.

Nel's gaze swung unsteadily to her. "What? You want me to thank you? Get on my knees and kiss your Jimmy Choos? You showed up a week too late and waving your big shiny business card. I'm not going to thank you. My site is shut down. My site manager—my best friend, may I remind you— was murdered last week. It wasn't a fucking accident and the guys who did it have been vandalizing our stuff all season. I've got shit to do, woman, and none of it involves you."

"I get that you have a lot to deal with, Nel. So would you care to tell me why you're drunk at ten in the morning?"

Nel made a point to slam the screen door especially hard as she left the bar.

Nel was certain death-hangovers were far worse than their alcohol counterparts. Her head pounded from weeping and she managed to pull a muscle during her jukebox dancing the day before. The countertop was cool against her forehead and her stiff hands clutched her empty coffee like a lifeline. She set the coffee to steep, but couldn't bring herself to get up to pour it. She didn't move when soft footsteps entered the kitchen. They paused in the doorway, their owner clearly surveying the destruction that was Nel. The refrigerator door opened, closed, and then Nel heard the gurgling hiss as the French press was depressed.

A warm hand gently pried the empty mug from her hands, replacing it with a steaming one a moment later. "Milk or sugar?"

"Milk." Her voice was a rock star's croak. She pulled her eyes open and peered through the coffee's steam at the woman. She wore something that was either elegant travel clothes or the most expensive pajama's Nel had ever seen. "It's Lin, right?"

"It is. I've got the room just below yours."

Nel looked back at the coffee. It was the perfect color. The ghost of a smile flitted across her mouth. "Thanks for this." She took a tentative sip, allowing the scalding liquid to erase the sense that something had crawled in to rot atop her tongue. "What's the agenda for today?"

"You run this gig."

"Right, but you must be here for a purpose."

"Correct. I wanted to meet your crew chiefs and examine the site and the artifacts. Just bring me up to date." Her gaze brushed over Nel's appearance. "It can wait till you're fully awake, though." The words and expression were not judgmental or cruel, but their honesty burned Nel's raw thoughts.

An hour later saw Nel tottering down the stairs. Lin sat gracefully at the counter, flipping through something that looked terribly legal and boring. She wore black jeans and a collared shirt that was only slightly too thick for a gala. Nel suddenly felt underdressed. "You want to go to the site first or check out the artifacts?"

"Site. I like to get the big picture first." She glanced at Nel's tank top and cargo shorts. "Will we be hiking?"

Nel flushed. "No, this is just how I dress."

Lin seemed unfazed. "I'll grab some water and meet you at the Jeep in five."

Nel turned down the back hall and slammed through the door. Lin was kind, but something about the woman irked Nel. Her hands acting without thought, unlocking the shed and climbing into the Jeep from the back. She had it backed out and idling in the drive when Lin stepped out. The tall woman swung herself in easily, flicking back her braid. "Who found the site? The survey was two years ago, correct?"

"Yeah. We did a walk over the year before based on a tool found during a raw-material hike. I wrote my dissertation on how bias against atypical site locations can hinder the discovery of sites in abnormal locations."

"It was decent, if a bit pretentious."

Nel glanced over. "You read it?" Her eyes narrowed. "Pretentious? Who's the one who wore a suit into a tiny Chilean bar?"

Lin's mouth quirked. "There are different kinds of pretentious. Your strength of conviction is not easily translated for those less intense than you or I."

Nel glanced between her and the road a few more times, eyes narrowed. "Fair enough. Perhaps I should begin with how much you know about the site. Are you an archaeologist?"

"Anthropologist. This is actually part of my fieldwork and dissertation. I know that you think this is one of the earlier sites in the country. You were excavating to find lithic evidence of occupation and to determine the technology used. What have you found? Diagnostics? Structures?"

"Diagnostics. We have both fluted and fish tail points."

"Are you of the belief they were the only group to prehistorically inhabit South America?"

"Certainly not. I think they were here, but I think groups also came from Southeast Asia. There's even mitochondrial DNA evidence to support that."

Lin grinned.

"What?"

"It's refreshing to talk to someone so intelligent and passionate."

"Thank you." Nel faltered, unsure what to do with the compliment. "Anyways, this one's early. It seems to be a hunting and fishing outpost. Lots of debitage, but no structures, save for one that is completely puzzling. I'll explain that when we see it. The site is located by a stream that spills into the ocean, but it's tucked into a hill, so its protected from the winds."

"Can I build my house here?"

Nel laughed. "I always determine whether or not I think a site's somewhere by whether I'd want to live there."

"People's tastes haven't changed much in the past 20,000 years, I'd imagine."

"I think our tastes are so ingrained, we just make new reasoning as to why things speak to us— a beautiful view could provide a lookout for hunting or warfare. Same with the people we find attractive." The Jeep lurched off the highway and onto the access road. Nel popped into second gear and forced the vehicle to grumble up the hill. She had not been back to the site yet. She didn't know what to expect or whether things would look different from the week before. *Mikey's gone. The entire world looks different.* The Jeep shuddered to a stop and she turned it off. Silence bloomed in the wake of the engine's rumble. Nel flung the door open and forced her boots onto the ground before she could change her mind.

Insects buzzed and the soil crunched as Nel trudged onto the site. She scanned the landscape, but didn't let her eyes rest on anything for too long. If she did, all they would see would be absence. "Alright, so when we did the walk over, the surface finds were concentrated around the western edge of the site. We thought they might be eroding out of the hillside, but a few tests later showed us that they were coming from this little valley." She pointed out the grid and explained what had been found in each unit and what she thought could be made of the information. She was aware of her voice humming in her ears and that she responded to Lin's questions. She didn't know what words came out of her mouth.

Nel jerked her head at the eastern half of the site. "We found the burial and those odd rocks this way, if you want to see them. Thank goodness we got everything out before we got shut down."

"I think I've seen enough, actually." Lin smiled. "I'm going to talk to my boss tonight, but I bet you a beer I'll have you back here next year."

Nel's laugh puffed through her sunbaked lips. "I'll believe that when I see it. You said you wanted to meet with Chad?"

Lin nodded, the gesture regal from her sleek head. "The rest of your crew are no longer in the country, I assume."

"The students are all gone. Chad drove them to the airport the day you arrived. He'll be back from Antofagasta this afternoon, though. He's my other experienced digger."

"Nel?"

Nel hummed questioningly.

"I'm going to find a hill or bush to pee behind, I'll be right back."

"Don't piss on the stream." Smiling felt stiff, like her face was made of tanned leather. She paused, midsentence, and stared at the lunch-box forgotten in the corner of the pop-up. It wasn't Mikey's. That would have been too perfect—a memento left for her to find.

"Nel, I found a trowel over by that pile of rocks." Lin held out a worn Marshaltown. "I assume it's one of the crew's?"

Blood roared in Nel's ears and her eyes tunneled. The handle of the trowel was carved with intricate swirls and a design of a Clovis point. Her instinct was to grab it from Lin's hand, wipe anything tainting the wood of the precious tool. "That's Mikey's. He called it Dirt-o-mancer."

Lin's brows rose and she handed it carefully to Nel. "Does that make it evidence?"

"Like fuck. I'm not giving them this. I know who killed him and they're not going to even consider it." She pressed the warm wood to her lips with reverence. Finally she trusted her voice not to crack against the lump in her throat. "I'll meet you at the car."

"You need help packing the equipment?"

"No, I'll do it tomorrow when Chad's here to help. I just need a few minutes alone." She listened to Lin's quiet steps retreat to the car. Though she had been to her share of funerals, grieving made Nel uncomfortable. "Closet griever," her father called her. Now her heart aches, as if it saved every ounce of grief for this moment. She hiked up the hill to the south. The burnt earth dropped toward the water. The ocean was brilliant under the sun. Archaeologists seemed to only look at the ground, searching for artifacts. Mikey had reminded her more than once to look up. Nel turned slowly, taking in the view. To the east battered trees clustered along the river's edge, clinging to the faint trace of life in the desert. The heat haze from the Atacama was visible even from her perch on the hilltop. A condor spun lazily in the thermals.

Her throat closed too tightly for her to swallow her tears. She lifted her face and let them come.

TWENTY

Chad was unpacking groceries when Nel and Lin returned. "Hey, I wasn't sure how long we'd be here for, so I didn't bother getting a ton of stuff, just enough for the week." He turned and stopped, black brows arching in curiosity. "New friend?"

Nel shrugged. "Chad this is Lin Nalawangsa. She's from our backers. Came to check on the site and all, considering the recent events. Lin, this is Dr. Chad Calligaris."

Chad leaned across the counter to offer his hand. "Pleasure, Ms. Nalawangsa."

"Lin's fine."

Nel edged around the island to grab a beer from the six-pack on the counter. It was only after her second long pull that she caught Chad's expression. "What?"

"It's one in the afternoon, Nel."

"It's not like we have work."

"You still have to show me the artifacts, Dr. Bently." Lin took the glass of water Chad offered her and nodded her thanks.

"They're upstairs. It's not like I have to drive." She headed towards the stairs. Something about Lin made her skin crawl. It wasn't deep enough for her to outright dislike the woman, but it irked her. *It's like she doesn't quite fit. She walks the walk, talks the talk, but it's something out of the corner of my eye.*

"I know I'm not what you expected or wanted, but I do think your work here is good and I respect your methodology."

Nel glanced back. *Great, she's a fucking mind reader.* "You're fine. I'm just not really a people person." She tugged the cardboard boxes from the shelves and tossed their tops aside. "We got a few good artifacts and plenty of debitage." She handed baggies of tools to Lin.

Lin tapped the paper envelope. "You were planning on doing protein analysis?"

"Yeah. I was able to run one on our intact tool, actually. Got the results back last week." She flipped through the paperwork to find the copy of the results. "Came back with human. It was associated with the burial, as well."

"You think it was the weapon that killed them?"

Nel shrugged. "There were only bones left, it'd be hard to tell now. It wasn't within the staining, so I know it's unlikely that the point was imbedded at the time of the burial."

"Killers have been known to bury the weapon with their victims."

Nel hummed noncommittally. She still wasn't sure what to make of the burial or the results. *This whole site is fucked.* "The concentration of artifacts is definitely in Block X. There was virtually nothing in Block Y, save for the burial. The test pits I laid in between the rock walls were negative as well, though the strats were unusual."

"Unusual how?"

"There was a black layer bisecting the B horizon."

"Burn layer? Volcanic activity?"

"It wasn't volcanic ash. It came back with all sorts of readings." She fought back a yawn and slumped into one of the chairs. The previous week barreled down on her with menacing weight.

Lin flicked on the desk's lamp and drew up her own chair. She put on a pair of steel-grey readers that looked far too thin to do any actual good. "Are the readings in here?"

"Yeah, towards the back." Nel propped her chin on her hand, watching the other woman flip through the results. The light was soft and the sun from the window warmed the room comfortably. A fly *buzz-tapped* its way up the glass. Nel's eyes slid into an unfocused stare, trailing the lines of Lin's face absently. The black line of a hidden tattoo poked from the back of her shirt collar.

There was something about the woman, something that slid from Nel's gaze and thoughts just as she was about to name it. *She doesn't belong.*

Nel's chin slid from her hand, waking her with a jolt.

Lin glanced over, brown eyes softening slightly at Nel's disheveled appearance. "I'm sure I can find my way around the paperwork. Why don't you rest a bit? I can have Chad walk me through it."

"He's down at the precinct I think." Nel straightened with a sigh. She was exhausted but this was her work, her site, not Chad's. "Do you mind if we revisit this later?"

"Not at all. How about over dinner?"

"Sure." Nel rose and started packing away the artifacts. "If you'd like, you can look over the paperwork tonight."

"I'd like that." Lin's gaze narrowed as she took the folder. "Are you alright?"

"I'm fine." Nel closed the door behind them. "Just exhausted." She listened to Lin move quietly down the stairs and into her own room. A horrible combination of anxiety and exhaustion warred for her brain. *I really shouldn't drink when I'm like this.* She crawled into bed, not caring that her clothes were sweaty and her boots still on. The wooden handle of Mikey's trowel was warm in her hand. She closed her eyes. "Why the fuck did you have to be the one they took?"

The knock on the door was just as polite and crisp as Lin herself.

Nel opened the door, scraping her hair back with a frustrated sigh. "Yeah?"

"I'm sorry, did I wake you?"

"No I always look like this." Nel glowered at the snowy collared shirt and grey jeans. "What did you need?"

Lin shifted her weight to the other black ballet flat. On a less poised woman the gesture would have seemed uncertain. "You said we could look over the maps at dinner."

Nel glanced at the clock. 7:00 on the nose. "Right." She opened the door wider. "Come in."

"I threw a little something together." She held up a tray and eyed the messy surfaces around her. "Is there someplace I could put this?"

"Sorry for the mess." She brushed crumbs and various writing utensils onto the floor to clear a spot for the food.

Lin pulled the dishtowel off the tray and handed Nel a plate. "Are these maps from your survey?"

"Yeah, updated with current GIS, topo, and our grids." Nel dug her fork into the mound of curry. "This is awesome, thanks." She jerked her chin at the maps, talking around a mouthful of food. "I don't know what they told you, miss 'liaison,' but this site is fucked up. Even before Los Pobladores ever got their teeth into it. The strats are all wrong, there're hydrocarbons in the B and someone shit metal dust all over this weird-ass landform, which, by the way, is flatter than my tits."

Lin leaned against the desk, slipping on her readers again. She didn't seem to notice the red-brown line of dirt the desk's edge left on her shirt.

Nel eyed her. *This woman is* made *of money.* "It's nonsense to most. See these," she pointed to the red X's, "are—"

"Where you took GIS readings. I know how to read a map, Nel. I wasn't born in these clothes, you know."

Nel frowned. *That was uncanny.*

Lin's mouth twisted. "These readings are all right. Did you notice anything about the landform?"

"Yeah. Mikey-" She cleared her throat. "Mikey said it looked like a sluice way, but down on the habitable strata it's flat."

"They look fine to me."

"What, the readings?"

"No, your breasts."

Either she has one hell of a dead-pan, or she's being serious. Nel shifted awkwardly. "What do you make of the data from the burning?"

Lin deftly rolled the map to the side to peer at the profiles of the STPs Nel placed between the two lines of rocks. "This thin layer here?"

"Yeah. The data came back all fucked—hydrocarbons and magnetized shit. It's contaminated, but I have no clue how. The strats are as intact as the rest of the site, which pisses me off to no end because I can't even use the data for the site itself if this is contaminated."

"I think your mind has been narrowed too much by academia."

Nel's sun-bleached brows shot up. "I haven't been out of the field a whole year yet."

"Right, but when people have to worry about publishing reports in peer-reviewed journals without being strung up, they lose their passion and bright ideas. For a good reason, I know, but it's a shame." She finally picked up her own plate and began to eat.

Nel bent over the profiles, smoothing a calloused hand across the paper. "You're saying I missed something."

"I'm saying you're not letting yourself see something."

"And you won't tell me what it is."

Lin smiled, the expression maddening and sweet all at once. "You'll see it eventually. You're smart."

Lin offered a thin envelope. "Before coming here I stopped to see Dr. Danilo Salinas in Antofagasta."

"He works in Santiago."

"He was coming back from doing some testing for ALMA in San Pedro. Regardless, I was able to get my hands on your carbon dates." She smiled. "I think you'll want to see them."

Nel rolled her eyes, but snagged the envelope from her. "There was shit all over the place, I'm betting that report will tell me this is a site from the 2000s."

Lin shrugged one shoulder and slid it across the table. "Give it a chance."

Nel shot her a skeptical look before flicking a pocketknife open and slicing the envelope. She scanned the page, flipped it over, then scanned it again. "12,000 YBP? This can't be right."

"He said it was unusual, but he wasn't surprised." Her smile broadened. "This site has a lot to tell you, Nel. You just have to start listening."

"Sorry, Lin, but most of what I'm hearing lately is just bullshit."

TWENTY-ONE

Chad turned the Jeep off at the end of the access road, but didn't get out. He stared at the wheel for a moment before looking over at Nel. "Have you been back to the site? Since it happened, I mean?"

Nel refused to meet his eyes. "I was here when Lin looked it over."

"But you were performing then. You had your tough-girl mask on."

"I don't have a mask."

"Nonsense, Nel. Everyone does. And just because it's a mask doesn't mean it isn't real." He reached over and took her hand. "Yours is this badass, driven, woman that never compromises, never weakens, never cries. But there's more underneath. Someday you're not going to recognize yourself, though."

Nel stared at her hands, clenched in her lap. She already didn't, sometimes. "I didn't think I was a griever. I didn't think I was a crier."

"Your best friend is dead. Weeping isn't weakness." Chad squeezed her hand.

"I did cry. Lin gave me a few minutes alone." So why did she feel like tears still threatened? "I'm mostly just angry."

"You're always angry, but you're going to have to learn how to actually feel." He nodded towards the site. "Come on, let's clean this place up. Nothing will tire out your rage like backfilling an entire grid."

She managed a smile. "I bet I can do it faster."

"You're on."

Nel banged the door open, running a hand through her mop of hair. "Fuck, I smell bad enough to fell an elephant." She turned to see Lin perched on a stool, a tall glass of something clear before her. "Sorry, Lin, I don't mean to be so distractingly sexy."

Lin's gaze flicked from her book to Nel. "You're filthy."

A sly smile curled Nel's mouth. She leaned back, propped on the counter top. Dirt tumbled from her forearms. She cocked her hip, tank top riding up and showing the band of her boxer-briefs. "Oh, come on, you can't tell me you've never seen a woman get dirty."

Lin's expression was forcibly unreadable. "I've seen archaeologists come out of the field without looking like they slept in their units."

Nel shoved herself away from the counter and sauntered toward the fridge. "Then they were doing it wrong. We're feral—we're not meant to be clean. Besides, we were backfilling." She pulled out the lemonade and poured herself a glass before adding more than enough tequila. After a few deep gulps, she set the glass aside and crossed her arms. "Thank you."

Lin's gaze had returned to her book. "For?"

"For overseeing this yourself. It means something that you came to try and reopen the site in person." She shifted her weight. "I know this is probably not your idea of a dream assignment, and I can only imagine what you're writing home to your girlfriend. But thanks nonetheless."

Lin closed her book carefully and pushed it aside. She folded her arms on the counter and leaned forward. "Nel, for someone whose world just got turned upside down, you're awfully quick to assume. You know nothing of who sent me here or why I requested this assignment. I'd love to have a chat about it, but maybe a conversation that has less snide judgment." Her lips quirked just enough to soften the hard words. "Care for a drink?"

Nel's grin broadened. "Your treat?"

"Surely you can pay, considering your funding's back."

Nel snorted and headed for the stairs. "I guess I'll go shower."

"You'd best. Wouldn't want to upset the other diners with how distractingly sexy you are."

Nel toweled off her hair in front of the mirror. She usually threw on anything, but this felt different. She and Lin danced around each other, both vying for power like it was a drug. Nel had always loved alpha women, and Lin was a whole new breed. The collared shirt was old and a bit faded, but it looked damn good over her dressier pair of men's jeans. She dug out an old bolo tie from grad school and tossed it around her popped collar. She even traded her work boots for her old pair of Frye boots. *Am I trying to impress her because she's badass or because I want in her pants?* Nel grinned at her reflection in the mirror. *Either way, I look good.*

She took the stairs two at a time, reveling in the familiar clomp of her soles on the worn wood. Of course, Lin already waited at the counter. She looked like she hired a team of stylists. Nel's confidence tripped on the last stair as she caught sight of Lin. *I wonder if she's trying just as hard.* She pulled a lazy smile onto her face and jerked her head at the door. "Mind walking?"

Lin fell into step beside her, her long legs making up for Nel's broad strides. "So are you planning on going to the same bar?"

"It's my favorite. Did you have something fancier in mind?"

"Fancier? Why do you think I'm a debutante?"

"You just feel cultured. Besides, you're dressed nicely."

"As are you."

Nel raised her hands in mock surrender. "Point. I thought it'd be best if we matched. They can think we're celebrating as opposed to you being kind enough to take a homeless woman out for dinner." She held open the screen door for the taller woman.

Lin laughed, a genuine, soft sound. "I'm sure no one would actually think that. How's this?" She pointed to two empty seats at the bar.

Nel shrugged. "Looks great. I knew a woman who had someone toss change into her coffee cup on the T. She was wearing her field clothes and had a bad day. They thought she was panhandling. At least it was Starbucks they ruined." Nel waved Jerod over and ordered her usual.

"Scotch, please." Lin turned back to Nel. "You've got style." She leaned forward, peering at the bolo. "Is that an artifact you're wearing around your neck?"

Nel lifted the point for the other woman to see better. "No, it's something a friend of mine made. I had another friend who dabbles in jewelry wrap it for me."

Lin glanced up without pulling away. "It's the same brown as your eyes."

"Munsungan chert, heat treated. It's a paleo raw material from the north-eastern U.S. I've never encountered it myself, but the color went with my theme."

"Earth tones?" Lin's hand was still nestled at Nel's collarbone.

"Dirt tones." Nel pulled away. Lin confused her. She was strong and fun, but had the power to rip Nel's work apart. *I've had enough fucked-up shit the past two weeks to last me a lifetime.* Mikey's absence was a steady ache that sharpened each time Nel turned to talk to him. Lin was a fun distraction, but Nel guessed that was all she would be. "So what's your dissertation on? Why'd you pick this?"

"I'm studying the culture of modern archaeology in relation to other similar professions. I thought a site continuously in danger of vandalism was just the ticket."

"A site that is now part of a murder investigation?" The words were biting and Nel didn't care.

Lin looked down at her own drink with a soft sigh. "My timing wasn't ideal. I've had some politics to wrestle."

Their drinks arrived and Nel took a long sip to hide the awkward silence. "You grew up here?"

"No, little remote place. My brother and I learned Chilean Spanish young, so it comes easily to me."

"You're close?"

"Closest. I haven't been home to see him in a long time though."

Nel stared at the swirls of mixing alcohol in her glass. "You must miss him."

Lin glanced up, her gaze heavy and clear on Nel's face. "Tell me about your friend—Michael Servais."

"Mikey. Everyone called him Mikey. I've known him since undergrad. I drunkenly hit him up at a bar for a classmate that was too shy. She broke his heart and I got a best friend. Kindest heart I've ever met."

"He was a teacher too?"

"Better than I could ever be. He has that gentle patience that's so important. I think the school would rather he be head of the prehistorics department, but he won't apply for it. He liked teaching, not bureaucracy."

"And you do?"

Nel shrugged. "I'm not a fan of people in general."

Lin's laugh was slow and easy. "I wish I'd met him."

Nel snorted. "He would have spent the whole time trying to set us up."

Nel ghosted down the stairs. She couldn't sleep, even after two hours of drinking at the bar. She paused on the last landing, eyes narrowed. The dim light over the kitchen island was on. She padded into the hall and peered around the door.

Lin sat with her back to Nel, peering at the blue glow of her laptop screen. Nel rolled her eyes. Lin may have been growing on her, but she still wanted the kitchen to herself in the morning. She slid onto the stool beside the other woman, glancing at the screen. Next to an x-ray of a clavicle and cervical vertebrae was an image of bloody asphalt. "What're you looking at?"

Lin clicked the computer shut. "Dr. Servais' autopsy report was just filed. A colleague of mine got a hold of it for me."

Nel's stomach lurched. *That was blood. That was Mikey's blood.* "Let me see it."

"I really don't think that's a good idea."

"Let me fucking see it." Her blood pounded in her ears. A chasm yawned in front of her thoughts, a dark pit of grief and uncertainty she was not ready to face.

Lin sighed and slid the computer across the island before standing by the fridge. Nel pushed the laptop open. "What's your password?"

"Starfall, capital 'S' and no spaces."

Nel flicked through the x-rays. Broken clavicle. Broken neck. Crushed temporal plate. Shattered knees and left tibia. She pressed her knuckles to her mouth, teeth digging purple crescents into the skin. Her stomach was a pit of snakes.

The autopsy was standard. Stark lighting turned ligature into bloody purple blossoms. Mikey's hair was too neat, the curls combed back against his head.

The kettle's scream snapped her from the autopsy room to the house's kitchen.

"Are you alright?"

Nel swallowed hard, once, twice. She cleared emotions from her throat. "I don't know."

Lin slid a mug of coffee across the counter.

Nel was suddenly grateful that the other woman refrained from an "I told you so." She drew a shaking breath.

"I think I'm going to file some of the artifacts." She pushed away from the table and moved up the stairs. Her face may have been blank, but her thoughts whirled. She had seen those injuries before. She shut the door and briskly stowed the artifacts still on the desk. She ripped the sheet from the bed and draped it over the bare desk before retrieving the burial remains. The bones were soft, too light to be stone, too hard to be wood. She gathered the several bags that were flagged. The red tag denoted the bones within had peri- or ante-mortem damage. She laid them out anatomically, her hands shaking. She didn't see weathered, brown bones. She saw a ski-jump nose and the slight surprise of a scarred eyebrow. The worn remains before her didn't make a person. They were an echo of the space he or she had once occupied, but they weren't a human. The photos of Mikey were just as hollow. It was as if all the pieces of a favorite toy were reassembled without the stuffing.

She pulled out her field book and sketched a roughly anatomical stick person. She mentally applauded herself for paying such close attention during her osteology courses. Double lines denoted a broken clavicle. Chipping on the C2 may have been from a blunt blow.

She continued through all the bones that were clearly damaged. The injuries were uncannily similar to those on Mikey's autopsy report.

Chad's patterned knock startled a gasp from her. "Hey, I'm throwing together some lunch, want any?"

"I'm not hungry, thanks though."

He paused, the floor outside creaking as if he debated entering. "Lin said you might need a bit of time. I'll call up when it's done if you want some."

Nel hummed, not really hearing. She did not hear the stairs mutter under his retreat nor Lin's polite call that dinner was ready hours later. By the time Nel looked up, it was fully dark and her eyes ached from squinting.

TWENTY-TWO

Nel wasn't religious. Still, soul or no soul, whatever had been Mikey, her laughing, sweet, Mikey, was gone. She pressed a hand to the glass that separated her from the cold body on the other side.

The door to the police precinct's viewing room clicked shut. "They said you were in here. Do you want to be alone?" When she jerked her head, Chad's hand slid over hers, warm and dry. "I'm so sorry."

"His hair's wrong." It was a stupid thing to care about, but she was clinging desperately to the slivers of reality that still made sense. She had wanted so badly to see Mikey's body, to prove, somehow, that he wasn't really dead. "He was never afraid of dying, Chad. He told me once that if he had to believe in a traditional idea of afterlife, he would choose reincarnation. Said the atoms that made him were once a thousand different things, and when he was gone, they would become a thousand more. I can't help but worry he was afraid at the end."

"Chad said I could find you up here."

Nel glanced over her shoulder. With jeans and a tee, Lin could almost fit in. "Yeah, it's kind of my spot. Quiet up here."

Lin faltered. "You want me to leave?"

"Nah, you're fine." Nel slid over on the ledge. "You want a beer?"

Lin plopped down beside her and held up a make-your-own sixer. I'm set."

"So you don't only drink scotch?" Nel peered through the choices. "These aren't bad. A bit dark for my tastes, but the class is there."

"Class is always there."

Nel passed her the bottle opener, watching the long fingers pry the metal loose. The nudge in the back of her mind came again. "So why are you here? Really?"

Lin pulled a strand of her dark hair from its bun and wove it absently through her fingers. "There are so many reasons. Tiny little choices that we don't even realize we've made until we look back."

Nel glanced over. "Whoa there, Socrates. I meant, like, why did you come here?"

Lin laughed softly, though the serious expression barely dimmed. "I know what you meant. It just occurred to me what *really* brings us places can be different from what we think."

"I think you had a few shower-beers."

She cocked her head. All the loose strands of hair drifted around her shoulders, the breeze curling them into tentative questions. "Shower-beer?"

"You really aren't from around here. Shower-beer is when you drink a cold beer in a hot shower. Best after a long, hot sweaty day in the dirt and sun." Nel leaned back against the plaster roof. It was rough through the thin cotton of her tank, but still warm from the sun. Her head flopped as she turned to look at Lin. The other woman's eyes were fathomless and dark, the irises dotted with grey and brown like galaxies in the night sky.

"Sounds a bit delicious."

"More than a bit." Nel's mouth was suddenly dry, and the bottle in her hand was empty. She really didn't want to sit up. Instead, she lifted her chin a bit, as if imparting a secret. "Why are you really here? What myriad unknown choices did you make to wind up on a rooftop in Chile, drinking with me?"

Lin's thin mouth curled into a smile, her eyes lidding. "You'd never believe me if I told you. What about your choices?"

"I'm really not sure. Could have been one, could have been a thousand." She swallowed carefully, chewing thoughtfully on her lower lip. "Really, the only choice on my mind is whether or not I should kiss you."

Lin's smile deepened and glass ground on plaster as she pushed her bottle away. "Sometimes I think those are the most important choices."

"Well you're not running for the hills."

"Nope."

There was such a thing as grief sex, Nel assumed—touch that was a terrified attempt at filling a sudden yawning chasm in the chest. The chasm in Nel's was raw and rocks still rattled into the abyss. She wondered if this would only hurt her more. She licked her lips nervously and leaned forward. Lin's mouth was hungry and careful at once.

Nel's calluses caught on cotton as she slid her hand up Lin's waist, pulling her closer. Her head whirled as thoughts spun down some mental drain. There was no such thing as seeing stars, but kissing came close. Nel pulled away and pressed her brow to Lin's. Her panting breath was loud against the distant sounds of nightlife. The chasm in her chest roared, the emptiness swallowed anxiety and inhibition. "Thank you. I needed that."

Lin cocked her head. Her cheeks were flushed and her eyes over-bright. The corner of her shirt had rolled up over her ribs, exposing an odd tattoo up her waist. She tucked a lock of Nel's hair behind an ear. "You're beautiful."

"I don't ever make promises. I don't know what tomorrow will be like."

"Neither do I." Lin grinned. "No one ever does."

Her mouth was more searching against Nel's this time, her tongue questioning. Nel's arms wrapped around the other woman, hands dragging up her back, learning the dips and curves of a new body, an alien landscape under the cartographer of her palms. Her lips parted, answering with every vulnerability. Her nerves sang. Lin slid a hand into Nel's Carhartts. Her hand was slender, a perfect balance of delicate and deft. Nel's body burned, tiny bolts of electricity radiating across her skin from Lin's curling fingers.

She fumbled with the three buttons on Lin's jeans, breathless. "What the fuck, even your jeans have to be classy."

Lin's laugh was a soft puff of air in the hollow of Nel's shoulder. It was followed a moment later by a low gasp as Nel pressed her muscled palm against Lin's clit. Nel pulled away just enough to watch her face. Her cheeks flushed peach, lips parted, breath hitching at each press of Nel's rough fingers. Lin's eyes opened, hazed from darkness and sex. "I want you."

Nel shimmied out of her shorts, kicking them aside with dismissing ease. Another minute of work and laughter later, Lin's pants were tossed away. Lin pulled Nel on top of her, hands ghosting over her hips to grab her ass. Nel tucked a leg up under Lin's until their bodies pressed together, her hand pinned between them. Lin's skin shone under the starlight, pale gold against Nel's tan, smooth against rough concrete. Heat rolled across Nel's body at the sight. *This woman couldn't be more fucking beautiful.* She hooked an arm around Lin's waist, lifting the other woman's hips against her own.

Lin reached up, gripping the back of Nel's neck. "I love how strong you are." She dragged Nel's mouth down to hers and whispered against her lips, "Fuck me." She bucked her hips, capturing Nel's gasp with her own.

Nel gripped the low wall of the roof, a wicked grin blossoming as Lin reached up to brace herself. She fucked her grief away, erasing every second of pain with each rock of her hips. Her eyes were lidded, unfocused with pleasure. She pulled each gasp and moan from the other woman with desperate tenderness.

A shiver unfurled up Nel's body, pleasure following it a moment later as her muscles tap-danced their way through orgasm.

Lin's eyes flew open a moment later, pupils blown as she came.

Nel lowered her carefully, breath gasping through passion and laughter. "I'm sorry I just fucked you on a rooftop. Not my classiest of moments." She rested her forehead on Lin's chest

Lin laughed. "Perhaps not. It was hot, though." She glanced up at the sky. "It's almost eight."

"How do you do that?" Nel sat back, still entangled, to look at the stars. "You have somewhere you need to be?"

"No, I just thought we could shower and move this party down to your bed."

Nel's smile broadened, easing across her face. "I wouldn't mind tasting you."

TWENTY-THREE

"What do you think the meaning of life is?" Nel stared at her ceiling, body blissfully loose and sore on a level only sex could reach.

"Seriously? What kind of question is that?" Lin shifted and Nel was aware of the other woman's deep brown eyes on her. Lin scoffed. "You're serious."

"I met someone a while ago—not anyone I'd like to meet again, but he had a point. Said life was all about searching for home, all about roots and finding where we belonged."

"You disagreed?"

"You sound surprised."

"I guess I thought archaeologists were all searching for something. Who we are, where we came from."

"We're searching, sure, but I think it's more complex than that. I think we're looking for where we're going. We see where we were and where we are. Next step is the future."

"I doubt many in this field share your thoughts."

"I rarely do." She allowed herself a grin at the poor joke. "So what about you?"

"I think life is about finding our place—dreaming big and finding ourselves settled in those dreams. Where we belong, so to speak, but not where we've been."

"Where we're going."

"Yeah." Lin's eyes narrowed. "Are you disappointed?"

"In?"

"Yourself. For having the same idea about life as a suited-up broad from the big city."

"I never said that."

"Your eyes did." Lin laughed softly. "I think you would have been disappointed then, had you realized we're searching for the same thing."

"Yeah, maybe. I also realized that guy had a point though. We're sums of where we've been. Great or small, each piece becomes a part of us."

"Who was he?"

"The head of Los Pobladores."

"You had drinks with the man who organized the vandalism of your life's work. Shit, you're more complicated than I realized."

Nel's smile curled wickedly and she rolled over to straddle Lin's hips. "Too complicated for a suited-up broad from the big city?"

Lin's laugh rolled like distant thunder in summer, her head tilted back. "Nel, the myriad tiny things that brought me here, made me this, are far more complicated than you realize."

Lin was unconsciously graceful, like a runner, the kind of steady strength that outlasted the sun. She traced a finger down the tattoo on Lin's arm. She had seen earlier that it reached around her shoulder and up her spine. The awareness nudged at her thoughts again, persistent, but still able to be pushed away. "It's like nerves. Halfway between spider-web natural and wires. It's cool."

"Thanks. You have any ink?"

"None. No piercings, nothing. By the time I realized earrings didn't make me girly, I was twenty and it seemed pointless. Tattoos are gorgeous as long as the needle isn't anywhere near my skin."

Lin snorted. "Baby."

"Did it hurt?"

"Of course, but what you're really asking is how much. It burned, it stung, it tickled even at times. It was worth it, though. My brother has one just like it."

"Where'd you get it done?"

"Back home."

"Where's home?"

Lin rolled her eyes. "That's a conversation for later. I'm hungry—wanna grab a bite to eat?"

Nel allowed the subject to change without protest. She had enough secrets too, ones that would come out later, maybe, but not tonight. "Yeah, I'd like something to drink, too."

"Bar?"

"Let's head to Juan Pablos." She swung herself off of Lin's body and out of the bed, stretching. It had been a while since she was naked in front of someone, not counting skinny-dipping. The old insecurities were fading, replaced by the knowledge of her body's strength. *I'm not tall or buxom, but I've got killer muscle-tone.*

"You're striking." Lin had yet to get up, curled on her side, head resting on one crooked arm. "I like strong women with rough hands and skin that's seen some work and sun and weather."

"Basically a sailor. Or pirate." Nel tugged on her shorts and began digging through her bag for a tank that wasn't bloody with dirt.

"Shovel-pirate." Lin slid to the edge of the bed and fished through the clothes on the floor to find her underwear.

"I'm pretty sure those are looters. And I take issue with looters." Nel finger-combed her hair into order, smiling at the sweet, musky scent on her left hand. She grabbed her phone and leaned against the dresser to watch Lin braid her hair. Lin's fingers twisted the pieces into some beautiful order. "I never learned to braid. You make it look like magic."

Lin laughed. "My mom taught both of us. Said even if we had short hair, the skill might come in handy. I have yet to braid anything else, but I trust she's right." She glanced over as she wound the braid around her head. "I could probably do yours in tiny pigtails."

Nel grimaced and held the bedroom door open for her. "I'll pass. Besides, I prefer to style my hair with field-gel."

Lin led the way past the silent crew rooms and into the street. "And that would be?"

"The perfect mixture of sweat, bug-spray, sunscreen, and dirt."

"Sexy." Lin slid her hands into the pockets of her jeans, staring up at the sky. Nel's boots thumped a rumbled echo to the whisper of the other woman's sandals. "It's beautiful, isn't it?"

Nel followed her gaze. The night was quiet and clear, the stars incredibly bright, and the Milky Way a winding river against the void. "Yeah. Makes you feel small and big all at once."

"We're such a small, yet important piece to it all. Like the tiny microbes in the soil—unseen but integral. Makes me homesick, sometimes."

"The stars?" Nel tilted her heat at the woman.

"Yeah. All that emptiness with potentially millions of other worlds, all just as alone." Lin shrugged.

"Ever see the movie *Contact*?"

"If there aren't other worlds, other people, 'it'd be an awful waste of space.' That movie, and the scene on Vega, feels like my family's mantra." Lin smiled, but her eyes darkened with something close to sorrow.

"Dude, your family is the best." Nel ducked into the bar after Lin. The noise swelled, enveloping them like warm rain. "Grab a table, I'll get drinks. What're you in the mood for?"

"Something with bite. Surprise me."

Nel wound through the tables and leaned over the bar. "Hey, man. Two shots of cuervo, a glass of your shandy and a stout."

"Where you sitting?"

"Blue table by the window."

The bartender glanced over and grinned. "Got a looker tonight, eh?"

"Eyes, off, man, she's with me." Nel grinned and headed back to where Lin had found a two-person seat by one of the dirty picture windows. Partway across the room she caught sight of two figures on the other side of the street. After being held at gunpoint, she'd recognize Emilio anywhere. His face was lined and shadowed with more than night. Before rage clouded her thought, a tiny voice told her that it was regret that darkened the circles under his eyes. The other man's back faced her, but he nodded and jerked a thumb towards the bar. Emilio glanced up and met her gaze.

"Fuck this." Nel sprinted through the rear door of the bar, muscles unused since high school track meets grumbling awake. Adrenaline temporarily erased pulled muscles and screaming tendons. The morning would feel differently.

She pounded up to her room and grabbed her pack. Mikey was right to carry knives all the time.

All she had was a pocketknife and a 3cm blade wasn't much against killers. Her shaking hand found the worn handle of Mikey's Dirt-o-mancer. She momentarily congratulated herself on taking the time that morning to sharpen the tool. She tucked it into her back pocket with her cell and wallet before climbing up into the hills behind the house. She circled the town, listening for the sounds of a fight or commotion. Lin was smart, and Nel hoped the other woman knew enough to book it back to the house. *I should have told her to run. She shouldn't get caught up in this. She's clever, but this is different. Even I'm not rough enough to be ready for this mess.* The uneven dirt tumbled down-slope in the wake of her boots and she slowed. The restaurant was just a few houses away and the large shed just beyond. Nel's eyes burned with manic anger.

She gripped her trowel and eased herself down the hill towards the shed. The windows were blacked-out, but light glimmered where the paint had flaked from the glass. Her shoulders groaned as she lowered herself from the retaining wall silently. She pressed herself against the shed's sidewall, chest heaving. The night was cool and still. Goosebumps flared across her bare legs. *Should have grabbed pants.* There were dozens of "should have" thoughts tumbling through her head, but most were too serious for her to consider without panicking.

The wood at her back was dry and rough, splinters sliding through her shirt and skin. She forced herself to breathe through her mouth to stay quiet as she inched towards the window. If she could see in, they might notice the black of night outside becoming the pale of her shirt. *Should have worn my black one.* She crouched until she could peer in without pressing her eye to the hole in the paint.

Whatever she expected to see, it wasn't Lin holding a weapon at Bastian's head.

TWENTY-FOUR

"What the fuck?" The words were whispered, but she saw Lin's eyes flick to Nel's side of the shed. *There's no way she heard that. None.* Nel turned back to the front of the shed, hoping to find a way to burst in without getting everyone shot.

Emilio stood at the corner of the building. He was a black void in the stars scattered across the sky behind him. He slowly pressed two fingers to his lips. He reached out, one hand still raised in peace between them, and handed her a piece of paper. She scoffed silently when she realized it was one of the menus from his restaurant.

Your man was never meant to die. Bas has taken this too far. Come in and we can talk.

Nel's eyes narrowed. *This is getting weird. Too weird.* She glanced through the crack in the window. No one had moved, it was as if they waited for something. Maybe it was for her.

Finally, she nodded.

Los Pobladores headquarters was a glorified garden shed. Nel gave herself three seconds to glance around the room and she was fairly certain a weed-whacker and hoe hung in one corner. Bastian sat stiffly, his gun on the table before him, but out of arm's reach. Two others leaned against rear walls, but none seemed armed. "Hey, Lin." The casual words ground against Nel's forced tone. "Come here often?" *She's not one of them, based only on the fact that she's holding Bastian at ...weapon point?*

"Hey."

Nel's eyes fell to Lin's hand again. It was encased in metal and the kind of fabric Nel thought might stop bullets. Two slim metal bars rested snuggly over the lines of her strange tattoos. Her hand was outstretched, as if telling Bastian to stop, but the steel in her eyes was all feral menace. "Looks like you're better prepared than I am."

Lin snorted. "I wasn't the one who ran pell-mell into the dark without paying for our drinks."

Nel shifted. *Is she actually angry?* She was acutely aware of Emilio a step behind and to her side. "So you wanted to talk?"

Emilio made a low, lurching hiss.

Nel was too nervous to turn, but after a minute she realized he was laughing. "Seriously?"

"I want all of us to talk. This has gone far enough, we all agree. Can we put disagreements aside and discuss this?"

Adrenaline nudged Nel towards the mental chasm she had avoided for weeks. "Discuss what, exactly? As far as I'm concerned, you people dragged the best man I've known out onto a roadside, did fuck-knows-what to him, and gunned him down when you were done." Her words snarled through her clenched teeth.

"Not a good start, slinging blame," Bastian retorted.

"Actually, I think she got right to the point." Lin's voice was charged, all the threat of an approaching thunderhead. "Los Pobladores. The Founders. Deep Roots. Half a dozen names and you thought we wouldn't find you? You thought burying all our heritage under 60cm of dirt would keep us away?"

"We didn't bury it. Time does that you know," Emilio pointed out.

"I was told we'd be welcome. I was told we'd be expected. I thought the earth would be ready for us!" Lin's voice broke.

What the actual fuck? The nudge at the back of Nel's mind turned into a shove, a hurtling blow that made her dizzy. *Lin really isn't from around here.* "Lin, you're losing me."

"We can't do this now, Nel."

"You didn't even let your bar-fling in on who you are?" Bastian's eyes flicked to Nel. "And you—I thought you were supposed to be some great student of people."

"Prehistoric Archaeology and Lithic Technology," Nel growled.

"Whatever. How'd you not see how poorly she fit here?"

"Bas, that's quite enough." Emilio stepped carefully out from his place by the door. "It only takes one man and an ounce of fear to pull a trigger, Ms. Bentley. It was never my intentions when I took over Los Pobladores that someone die. Our organization was not one of violence, though it may seem so. We are dedicated—"

"To preserving the integrity and soul of our resources, both ancient and newfound, cultural and natural. I know your damned motto."

"Ah yes, but there is more you perhaps do not know. I know the people you study are rather far removed from us, by modern standards, but they told a story. Disagreements happen often, but sometimes they have far-reaching effects that we never anticipate. Thus it was with these people."

"How can you know this? I know their tools and their lifestyle, but little else and I've spent my life studying them."

"So have I." His eyes softened. "Perhaps without the same degree of academia or excavation, but I've studied that site as much as you. Tell me—the rock forms you mapped, the black layer in the strata, what have they told you?"

"That they manipulated their landscape, though less than it looks, since many of those stones were naturally deposited. The black layer may have been some catastrophic event, like a volcano."

"We both know that's not volcanic ash."

"I can't explain it." Nel's lips thinned. This was not something she had ever anticipated discussing with him, and the experience was decidedly uncomfortable.

"Nel, do you remember that conversation we had about the meaning of life?" Lin's reminder was gentle.

Emilio raised his brows. "Well, your pillow talk is rather more interesting than mine."

Nel ignored him. "Where we came from versus where we're going."

"Yeah. Perhaps you should ask Mr. Sepulveda to elaborate on his philosophy."

Nel narrowed her gaze on Emilio. "I fail to see how your philosophy is going to make this better. We're standing in a shed in rural Chile waving bizarre gloves and talking archaeology. This is like a fucking Indiana Jones movie, and I'm not keen on it."

"Hear me out?" It was a question. Nudging in its open insistence, but gentle.

There was something paternal in his eyes and it eroded the mental cliff edging the void before her. "Alright."

As she moved to sit, Bastian's chair scraped back. The table jerked as he flung himself across it, fingers scrabbling for the gun. Light flooded the room with the sound of a transformer blowing, and Nel blinked furiously. "What the fuck?"

Gunshots peppered the air and she dropped, blinking light-seared eyes. Bastian flung a chair into the confusion and Nel pulled herself to the wall, head low. Whatever the light had been caused the air to smoke. Her groping hand found a sandaled foot and she glanced up. Fire clawed up the opposite wall, backlighting Lin.

Nel stared. It was as if her life was suddenly an action movie. Lin was unrecognizable as the woman in Nel's bed hours ago. But people weren't characters, and unless someone was obtuse to an obscene degree, the light reflecting from the myriad facets of their beings inevitably shone through. The woman in Nel's bed was relaxed and soft, perhaps, but the intelligence and checked power had been there. The focus in her eyes as she brought Nel to orgasm was the same with which she flexed her fingers and fired her weapon.

The second wave of adrenaline burst through her nerves, thrusting her into the void. The world tunneled and she rose into a crouch. Years of pounding shovels into the ground powered her across the room. She collided with one of the men she didn't know and rose from her crouch, trowel clawed in her hand. The sharpened metal ground against flesh and something hard. *Did I just stab someone?*

Light and sizzling engulfed the tiny room again. The door was blocked by Bastian's snarling figure, gun held with the mania of a zealot. *Fuck, this is bad.* The fire eating at the side of the building spelled several death sentences and none were particularly pretty. *I should have left a note, I should have told someone where we were going.* On the tail of her concerns came another: *I should have gone home.* Emilio appeared, crouched beside Nel. "There's another way out the back. Grab your girl and follow me."

Nel glanced up at Lin skeptically. Her fingers fumbled over the other woman's free hand. She pulled herself up and called over the sharp retort of energy and bullets, "There's a way out!"

Lin's fingers gripped Nel's tightly and the shorter woman tugged her towards the door buried in the hill. Emilio jerked it open, ducking twice at the sound of gunfire. Nel pulled Lin in behind him. The door thumped shut and the *shhk* of a lock falling into place echoed in the sudden stillness. It was dark. The hall smelled of leather and metal, like a smithy.

"Emilio?"

"Here."

"Do they have a key?"

"No. It's with me."

"Good." Nel drew a steady breath. "Everyone okay?"

Emilio's voice was rasping, but not strained. "I think they got my arm, but nothing that will kill me. Hurts, though."

Nel squeezed Lin's hand. "Lin?"

"I'm fine. Adrenaline is wonderful."

Nel laughed. The sound felt strange in her throat. "I'm okay. My wrist hurts like a bitch from when I fell, but I think I'm just being a baby." She fell silent, blinking rapidly to acclimate to the darkness. It was hopeless. The hall was blacker than any night. "So now what?"

"The hall leads down. It's been here a very long time—almost as long as your site." The floor sounded like stone under Nel's boots. No one spoke, save for Emilio's whispered warnings about uneven flooring or low-hanging beams. It took the better part of fifteen minutes before the echoing of their footfalls changed.

Nel stopped. "We're in a big room. Or a cave." She focused harder, catching the faint sound of running water.

Emilio fumbled with something metal a few paces away. Light pierced the darkness. He held a large flashlight, one hand shielding his eyes from the sudden brightness. "There's another hall that leads outside from here."

Nel barely heard him. Her eyes were trained on the simple art covering the walls. "I've seen these before." She pulled out her phone and flipped through the pictures. "Here!" She held the phone triumphantly up to the wall. "I must have been looking at them upside down." It was a simple shape. It looked geometric at first glance. *Or if you're holding it upside down.* "This can't be what I think it is." It was oblong, lines radiating at slight angles from three sides. The curls from the bottom and rear were like the lines used in comic to designate motion. She pointed angrily at the nearest one with her trowel. "Lin, why are there cave paintings of a fucking spaceship? If you tell me goddamned aliens are responsible for this, I'm fucking done."

A soft noise echoed through the cave. Nel turned, frowning, to see Lin doubled over, smothering her uncontrollable laughter with a hand. "Don't tell me you brought a sharpened trowel to a gunfight."

Nel's eyes narrowed, but the fight wasn't in her. She smiled, Lin's laughter worming into her and pulling a chuckle free from her chest. "Alright, this whole thing is ridiculous." She glanced at Emilio. "Can one of you enlighten me?"

Lin straightened, tears of laughter still clinging to her lashes. "I'd be happy to, but we have to settle this." She turned to Emilio. "We need to get to the site before the other Los Pobladores."

Nel's stomach clenched at the thought of what they might do.

"This tunnel leads out to the edge of town. It's not far from your house, but we've got to hurry. They'll catch on to where I've led you." He tucked the flashlight under his arm and edged past the paintings to another entryway. It was carved into the rock by water. The sound of water grew louder.

"Emilio, is this the same stream as the one in the pink cave?"

"It is. It runs through here all the way to the site and then to the ocean. There's a tunnel that reaches partway there, but for some reason it was never finished."

Lin squeezed Nel's hand before releasing it to trail her fingers along the wall. "It's stupid for me to question it now, but why the sudden change of heart?"

"Ah. Perhaps Nel, student of people, could answer that better than I." Emilio's brow rose, inviting Nel to answer.

Nel shrugged. "I don't know about that. You said you were tired of the fighting and that this wasn't how things were supposed to be. Is this what you referred to when we spoke about where we were going and where we've been?"

"It is, in part. This seems strange and impossible to you, but it has been the story on which I was raised. It is not impossible to me. Nor, I'd imagine, to Lin," he glanced back with a quiet smile, "though, perhaps we had different versions of the story."

Lin snorted. "Mine did not include a gunfight."

"Neither did mine. That is why I rethought my beliefs. They did not change, but the way I interpret the world may have." He stopped and handed Nel the flashlight. A wooden door stood before them. It looked identical to the one in the shed. "Hold this while I unlock it."

He fumbled for a moment, then the door swung away. After the darkness of the caves, the night seemed bright. A thin layer of clouds blocked the moon and stars. Nel stepped out with a relieved sigh. They were just over the hill from the house. She froze. "Emilio, we have company."

A line of men stood at the rise, unmoving, but clearly waiting.

"Run around the side and pick me up on your way back," Emilio offered.

"I wouldn't split up." Nel grimaced at the thought.

"I'm just going to talk to them." He shoved Lin after Nel and moved towards his former friends, hands raised.

Nel grabbed Lin's hand and pelted up the side of the hill, dreading the sound of fighting. They reached the gate of the house without mishap. The silence was almost worse than gunfire.

"Get the Jeep going, I've got to grab something." Lin bolted into the house, steps eerily silent.

Nel jerked a nod and unlocked the garage. She slipped the car into neutral and shoved off with her foot through the half-open door. It coasted through the shed doors and down the drive. Lin emerged as Nel passed the back porch. The tall woman swung herself into the passenger seat. The Jeep roared to life and Nel turned out of the drive.

The side of the road was deserted. The hilltop was empty. "Fuck, where is he?"

Lin sighed. "Nel, we got to go. They took him or killed him or something." Her hand found Nel's in the dark and squeezed. "Come on, we don't have much time."

TWENTY-FIVE

The Jeep rattled onto the dirt road, lurching over rocks Nel couldn't see in the dark. She glanced in the rearview and stopped the car.

"What are you doing? They could be there already." Lin twisted in her seat, peering down the stretch of road down which they had just escaped.

"I need some answers. Real ones."

"We're chasing a gun-wielding maniac and you might be charged with murder in the morning!"

"Exactly! Everything just got fucked up and I want to know what's going on. I'm practically blind here, Lin. Give me something."

Lin sat back, staring at her knees as if maybe they would answer the questions so she wouldn't have to. After a moment she looked up at the sky. "You know, sometimes there are these choices. They're choices that really suck, but they're important. Rock-and-a-hard-place choices. The world is in a bad way, and we've known we were heading here for a long time. My job is to bring you the tools to help. Problem is, some people don't believe in what we're doing."

"So, that kind of didn't answer anything. You talk like you're not a part of this world. Like this isn't your home." Nel pointed at the glove. "And you seem to think we're in a sci-fi movie."

Lin's laugh was dry and humorless. "Alright, say you were given one of those choices, but it meant leaving everything you knew and subjecting generations to a completely alien lifestyle. Well my ancestors made that choice. My brother and I grew up very far from here."

"Where?"

Lin looked up at the sky again, eyes bright. "You see that little blue-white star there?" She pointed. "Half way between here and there." They were silent a moment, then her eyes swiveled to Nel.

Nel's gaze was narrowed on the star. Suddenly her mouth curled and her shoulder shook with silent laughter. *That's it, she's batshit-crazy. She's a fucking loon, and here I am on the side of the road at night with her.* "Lin, what the fuck?"

"I know, proof. I sound like I'm nuts." She held out her hand. "This tattoo is conductive. It transmits electric signals from my brain to various devices on my hand. I've got other gloves, not just this one."

Nel glanced back at the road again. "So, assuming I believe you, which I really shouldn't, you're like an alien? What is this? I hate *Ancient*

Aliens and all that crap. Don't tell me the Mapuche didn't make their own culture."

"Of course, they did. And I'm not an alien. Well, not exactly. We're human. I mean, as human as you are. We lived on a ship with other humans and even another species for a time, though I never met them."

"And Los Pobladores dislike you because you sound like nut-jobs...?"

"Because we were charged with bringing technologic and biologic solutions to some of the issues you guys have made. Things you normally wouldn't develop for centuries."

"Why would you bother? Why would Los Pobladores want to stop you?"

"When the Emissaries first came to my ancestors it was thousands of years ago. Their technology and understanding of science would have seemed like magic, and humans weren't ready to wield that power. Besides, such gifts are best received from familiar faces. As for Los Pobladores, they don't think we need such tools. They think we're tainting what it means to be human. Perhaps over time, that small difference in opinion caused greater rifts than we realized."

Nel drew a steadying breath. "And who is 'we?'"

"The Earth-base of the Institute for the Development of Humanity. We realized humans hadn't been preparing for us. The place we were supposed to land was not maintained. It had to be isolated, safe, sacred. I've been on Earth for the past decade looking. I finally found this area and commissioned a survey from a driven, intelligent archaeologist. I think you know the rest."

"So we were digging up what, your air-traffic control?"

"Landing strip. The ship will navigate to this place with a magnetic field. We needed an electromagnet down here to pinpoint the location. It wasn't complicated until Los Pobladores went in and destroyed any semblance of peace we had."

"So why now?"

"Because I worry Los Pobladores will destroy it before I get the chance. They might have beaten us there." Lin eyed her sidelong. "Can you drive me to the site?"

"You know what they would do if they caught us there?" Nel whirled on her, glaring through the darkness. "I have a damn good idea. It involves beating you to death and leaving you on the side of the road."

Lin winced. "I'm sorry, Nel." She unbuckled her belt and hauled the duffle bag over her shoulder. "If I'm not back by morning, there's a letter on my desk. Send it. Then leave Chile and don't look back." She turned and started hiking up the access road.

Nel slumped into the seat. Adrenaline drained from her system and all she wanted was to cry herself to sleep. She didn't want to deal with aliens, or ancient space ships, or saving the world. *I'm not*

Indie. "Why now? Why me of all people." She scrubbed her face with a rough palm. She needed Mikey, she needed the rock that anchored her when everything else was uprooted. Her fingers traced the designs carved in the handle of his trowel. The summer had begun so well. Her own site, her own crew, her best friend laughing beside her.

Now she was alone on the side of a road, in the dark, being chased by madmen. *I'm not alone.* She looked up to where Lin had disappeared in the blackness of the access road. *"You're going to find someone badass and driven, someone who runs as fast as you do."*

Nel knew she was just as crazy as Lin, but she didn't care anymore. She slammed the Jeep into first. It didn't matter that Los Pobladores had guns and all she had was a trowel and a fuck-ton of anger. It didn't matter that she had no clue who Lin really was. They were running in the same direction.

The Jeep ground to a halt when Lin came into view. She glanced up at Nel, face half lit by the stars. Nel tugged the duffle bag from her grip and jerked her head at the hills. "Alright. Let's do this."

TWENTY-SIX

If the road was treacherous during the day, it was deadly at night. The wheels ground against rocks Nel forgot were there, and the oil pan scraped against the ridges more than once. Finally, they shuddered to a halt at the edge of the site.

"Fuck." Nel killed the engine and sat back. "This is gonna suck." Half a dozen figures stood arrayed across the entrance to the site. They were silhouettes against the star-studded sky, but Nel caught a glimpse of moon-lit armbands.

Lin's mouth thinned. "This might be more complicated than I hoped."

"What do you need to do? Not including kicking their asses."

"Those stones are magnetic. I need you to electrify this place."

"If you burn my goddamn site, I'll fucking kill you."

Lin snorted. "I wouldn't have anyways." She patted the duffel at her feet, never taking her eyes off the array of Los Pobladores. "I've got flares. Special ones. I need them attached to those rocks. All you need to do is flip a switch."

"Like a bomb?"

"Yeah, but I promise it won't screw up your stratigraphy." She shoved the bag into Nel's hands. "I'll distract them."

Nel glanced at the men, then back at Lin, then down to her glove-weapon. She tentatively offered her hand.

Lin took it and squeezed. "You ready?"

"Ready." Lin swung herself out of the Jeep, hand outstretched before her. "This is getting ridiculous, Sepulveda."

"You think I actually wanted this? You're less astute than I thought." Emilio's voice was low, woven with tension.

Nel watched as Lin approached. Emilio stood stiffly, arms loose at his sides. *At gunpoint, then.* "I didn't come to stop you, I came to help you. Clearly the rest of these imbeciles have other plans."

"Clearly you need to choose your company better. Duck." Without changing her tone, Lin swung her arm up, her other hand rising to steady her wrist as light and sound burst into the air. Nel clambered out of the Jeep, dragging the duffle behind her. She dropped to the ground and edged around the car. Los Pobladores may have been guarding the entrance, but she knew these hills as well as they did. The trek overland seemed to take forever, the boom of Lin's weapon echoing off the hillsides as the glow swelled then faded. Nel crested the hill and broke into a jog. The dirt was compact under her boots, and she only stumbled over rocks twice.

The ground flattened, the hillside spilling into the strange level area. *Guess what, Mikey? You were right. It does look like a runway.* She unzipped the bag and fumbled through the contents. The beacons were like the little solar lamps along the front walk to her father's house, except these were half Nel's height. It took several tries before she figured out how to embed them deep enough into the ground. The sounds of fighting had moved now, emanating from farther into the hills.

Her legs were tight from running and crouching, and up in the hills the air was crisp. She knelt, feeling awkwardly around the base of the rock, cold fingers pushing aside hard dirt, feeling for any imperfection. They paused on a thin pilot hole drilled into the stone. She cleared the soil away and shoved the metal rod of the beacon into the hole with a grunt. Tomorrow, she would look back on this and wonder what drugs she was on, but now she moved with single-minded determination. Nel hoisted the bag higher. Her back ached, and her arms were trembling. Whatever adrenaline she had was long spent. She stepped back, panting as she placed the last beacon on the northern line. *One side down, one to go.* Blasts and gunshots were replaced by shouts. She strained her ears, pressing her senses against the stillness, listening for Lin's low, clear voice. Nothing. She edged across the open area between the stones.

A figure burst from the darkness, rushing at Nel. She barely had time to crouch before he was on her. They tumbled to the ground, Nel jamming knees and elbows into what she hoped was a stomach.

"Bentley, you idiot, stop!" Emilio shoved himself away from her. In the darkness she couldn't see the glare, but his voice was thick with frustration.

She edged away, groping for the duffel as she went. "What the fuck, Emilio? You can't just rush me in the middle of a gunfight and expect me not to punch you!"

"Your punch leaves a bit to be desired." He dragged himself to his feet with a soft groan. "Your girl has quite the weapon."

"She hit you?"

"No, if she did I doubt I'd be as spry right now. I came to help."

Nel's brows rose. She should question it, but she didn't have the energy to take anything at more than face value. "Fine." She pulled three beacons from the bag and thrust them at him. "Feel for the holes in the bottom of the rocks. Spikes go in there."

She jogged further ahead, relying on her toes and shins to find the rocks for her. She ignored Emilio's soft laugh at her litany of curses and set to work on the next beacon. Half the holes were hidden by hard earth packed in for centuries. She slumped onto the ground beside the last one, staring at it, unseeing.

After a moment, Emilio sat beside her. She could smell sweat and blood, but wasn't sure whether it was his or hers, or someone else's entirely.

"So, do they start themselves?"

Nel shook her head and pulled the last piece from the bag. It was a heavy square of metal set with an old looking dial. She angled it towards the clouded moon, squinting. There was something off, just like when she looked at Lin. Something that slid through her mental fingers just as she grasped it. She rested a hand on it. "I'm sorry. This isn't how you wanted things to end."

He snorted and found her hand with his. "You're right. But I'm fairly certain this is not the end at all."

With the dry warmth of his hand over hers, she cranked the dial as far as possible. Her fingers fumbled then found the hard button at the base of the mechanism. She felt, rather than heard, a crackle, like a muted television. Light exploded across the site, searing her eyes and piercing up through the bank of clouds. "Fuck!" Nel blinked away light-marks on her retinas. She peered up at the sky through weeping eyes. Whatever light the beacons gave off, it wasn't normal. The clouds writhed away from the beams, like mist escaping dawn. "We better move. I'm not sure what comes next, but I'm done with being in the middle of the action."

Emilio nodded and pulled her to her feet. "The hills above the site, I'd guess."

Nel broke into a jog, navigating the terrain now that it was thrown into sharp relief. They were quiet, only the sound of boots on gravel punctuating their retreat. Even the shouts had faded now. Nel focused on their ascent, ignoring the insidious thoughts about why everyone else had fallen silent. Nel reached the crest of the hill, peering into the darkness at the corners of the site.

The beacons made it impossible to see whatever was in shadow. She cleared her throat. "Lin?" There was no answer, and Nel slumped to the ground, defeated and exhausted. She hadn't thought to ask what came next or what she was supposed to do if Lin was incapacitated. Emilio sat quietly beside her.

"I doubt she's injured, Bently."

Nel didn't answer. She just leaned her elbows on her knees and rested her head on her arms. Fatigue wrapped itself around her, muddling her thoughts into something that seemed like half a dream. The silence deepened. Emilio's gentle hand on her shoulder startled her back into alertness. Aching exhaustion was like a hangover, complete with a tight stomach. "How long was I out?"

"Twenty minutes, only." He nudged her and pointed out to the two rows of lights. "Lin's down there."

Nel leaned forward, blinking sleep and grit from her eyes. Lin stood at the mouth of the runway, one graceful hand shielding her face as she peered at the clouds. She checked her watch then looked up again.

Nel's stomach sank. "They're not coming."

He shushed her and pointed. The patch of clear sky writhed. Sound suddenly ceased as a wave of pressure swept across the site. A rumble followed, not something Nel could hear, but rather something that burst through her gut and left her weak. The air pulsed a second time, and a third. The dully glinting belly of some great metal craft nestled itself into the cleared pocket of sky.

"Holy fuck." Nel stood shakily, grabbing Emilio's shoulder as she teetered. A metal disc detached itself from the craft, lowering with a hum that was, again, more felt than heard. At first Nel thought she was seeing double. The figure standing on the disc was Lin's image, save for the lack of breasts. His bodysuit looked much like the glove Lin wore, and Nel was willing to bet he had tattoos that matched Lin's. The sleeveless robe reaching to his ankles should have billowed on his descent, but it remained eerily still. The disc halted a foot from the ground. He stepped off and raised a hand in greeting.

Lin closed the last few paces between them at a run. Their arms locked around one another for several minutes, and they murmured words that Nel could only guess. She swiped at cheeks suddenly wet and cold. She had no siblings but knew that if she could see Mikey again, their reunion would be identical.

Lin pulled away, hands waving as she spoke quickly. Her expression was too stern to be excited. Twice, her brother glanced up into the hills. Nel shuddered. It was impossible to see into the darkness with so much light around him, but his eyes seemed to meet hers. Finally, he shook his head. He handed Lin a thin tube. He cupped her face, kissed her brow, and stepped back onto the disc. The hum began and the disc rose.

"Dar, come back!" Lin's words cut through the sound of the spaceship, her voice cracking. She ran to stand under the ship, waving angrily.

He shook his head, then turned to look at Nel again. He pressed a fist to his chest then gestured out with an open palm. Finally he looked up as he ascended into the ship and the door sealed silently.

Lin screamed furiously, raising her gloved palm and firing two successive shots at the belly of the craft. "Damn you!"

Before Nel could think better of it, her feet were pounding down the hillside, skittering over loose rocks. She slid the last few meters down to the site. Pain lanced up her leg at the awkward landing. She hissed through her teeth and hobbled around the open units. She expected the light of the beacons to be warm, but they washed coldly over her. The electricity set her hairs on end. "Lin."

The woman didn't answer, snarling words Nel recognized only as curses.

Nel paused a step behind her. She steeled herself, then tentatively reached out and took Lin's gloved hand. She had not heard the conversation, but knew enough that something had gone wrong. "Come on. Let's go home. We can deal with it after we've slept."

Lin whirled on her, and Nel expected a shouting tirade. Instead her voice was hoarse and quiet. "He fucking left me here. I haven't seen him in a decade, and he left me here."

Nel brushed a long lock of black hair behind Lin's ear. "I know. I'm sorry." She tugged on the other woman's hand gently.

The pulse swept past, this time sucking air towards the ship. With the fourth pulse, the ship was gone. The beacons crackled into darkness. The sky was studded with stars. The night was quiet.

Lin jerked a nod and followed Nel unsteadily to the Jeep.

Emilio waited for them, leaning on one of the doors. "You appear to have shot my ride—mind dropping me at home?"

Nel didn't answer, only opened the rear door for him and climbed into the driver's seat. She didn't notice all the bumps and ruts on their way back down to the highway. No one spoke, wrapped in thought as their private worlds ended in a blast of light and silence.

TWENTY-SEVEN

Emilio squeezed Nel's hand, but did not speak as she let him out in front of his restaurant. Lin was silent until they stood under the luke-warm water of the shower.

"He said we weren't ready. He said tonight was a night for peace and alliances and awakening, and we only had bloodshed." Her breath hitched and she looked down. "I tried everything I could and failed."

Nel peered up into Lin's dark eyes. "I don't know what to say. I barely understand what just happened. But I don't think you failed. We failed. Humans failed. We're nothing if not stupid and stubborn and violent. Together we can be beautiful, but we can be terrible too."

"We had 14,000 years to be ready, what can I possibly do in twenty?"

"He's coming back?"

"Yes."

Nel wrapped her arms around Lin, careful of their collection of new bruises. "Then we'll get ready. Think of all that has changed in the last ten years. We're almost there, I promise." Lin rested her forehead on Nel's. They were too exhausted to weep, but Nel could feel her shaking.

"What if humans knew something was coming?"

"What do you mean?"

Lin pulled away. Her eyes held the clarity and honesty that only exhaustion brings. "I want you to publish your report."

Dawn came without mercy. All Nel had wanted to do was sleep, but it eluded her. She stared at the curve of Lin's back, watching the slow rise of her ribs as she breathed. The night before clattered into place in her mind. Her chest tightened with each event. They hadn't cleaned the site before leaving, and Nel had only the barest idea what was left. *Fuck, I think there are bodies.*

"What's wrong?"

Nel glanced over. Lin's back still faced her. "What?"

"You've been fidgeting for the last few minutes."

"I thought you were asleep."

"I thought you were. Think I could sleep after last night?"

Nel laughed softly. "Neither could I." She reached up and tangled her hand in Lin's hair. "I'm worried about what condition the site is in."

"Archaeologically, or otherwise?"

"We left beacons there. And bodies. And fuck knows what else."

"First thing tomorrow, we'll go clean up."

Nel laughed softly and tucked her head against the nape of Lin's neck.

"What?"

"It already is tomorrow."

Nel leaned back in the precinct chair. It seemed like years since she had last sat there, listening to the police refuse to pursue the truth. Now the anger and frustration faded into something else. *It's easy to think in black and white. Los Pobladores aren't all evil, and we aren't all good. Just like Lin said, each of us is the good-guy in our own story.* Munoz stepped in with a nod at her. "Thank you for your prompt arrival. We've reviewed the autopsy of your colleague Dr. Servais."

"Were you able to get any DNA off his wounds? His fingernails maybe."

"Despite what television tells us, it's rare we get so lucky, Dr. Bently. Our coroner reviewed the circumstances and compared it to his wounds. It seems we were wrong in our initial assessment. Dr. Servias was not murdered. He was struck by a vehicle on his way back from the site. We examined his car. The battery was dead. He must have left his lights running and needed a lift back to the Vicuña y Las Rosas. These back roads are dark at night and people often drive far too fast."

Nel's thoughts screamed through her head. *You're fucking kidding me.* "Where's your bulldog, Reyes? There's no way this was an accident. You wouldn't have assumed homicide without a good reason."

"Reyes has been called back to the city. I'm sorry that our actions upset you, Dr. Bently. We have Dr. Servais's personal effects, and are ready to release both them and the body to you. Have you made arrangements?"

"Yeah, I filed the paperwork and everything. I should be gone by next week. I'll call the funeral home now." She rose and fumbled her phone from her pocket as she headed toward the door.

"We'll be ready when they arrive." He paused at the door to their offices. "I'm sorry for your loss."

"Yeah. Thanks."

Nel took the stairs two at a time. She was panting as she shoved open her door. "Lin?" The silence was emptier than usual. She scanned the room, noting the lack of computer and clothing that had littered the floor that morning. "Fuck."

Nel wasn't big on goodbyes, but leaving without warning was just as shitty. She started to search for a clue, any sign that the woman would be back. Eventually her search ended in her tidying the room. Cleaning yielded a few pieces of paperwork and a shirt she had forgotten she brought. Her eyes narrowed on the box tucked under her pillow. *That wasn't there before.* She flipped it open. Inside nestled a bolo tie. The dark leather coiled beneath a metal object. Nel lifted it out carefully, angling it toward the light from her window. The metal was polished to a high sheen, the surface mottled with darker color and etched with a design she recognized. It was the same one her fingers traced down Lin's body.

A folded paper sat under the coiled leather. She sank onto her bed and unfolded the paper.

Nel

Sorry I left so quickly. Can't have a gunfight without involving the police, I suppose. I'm staying low for a while. Traveling, spreading the word. I was serious—I want you to publish your preliminary findings. There's so much more we want to share with the earthbound humankind and I know your study will help.

   -L

   P.S. This is a piece of space-rock, from your rocking space almost-girlfriend. I'll see you again.

Nel tucked the letter away. Everything was so surreal. Two weeks ago, she was leading a dig in the boonies of Chile with her best friend. Now, she had no friend, no site, and no almost-girlfriend. She wasn't ready to go home. Chile was like a vacation, even if she was working. Home meant returning to reality, one that should have Mikey in it. *Who knows if I'll ever be able to come back to this site again after what happened.* Regardless of what actually happened, she would be surprised if the feds didn't blame her for the mess. She draped the bolo over her neck and leaned back against the chimney. She cracked open her beer. "You were right Mikey. She's tall and fucking badass." She raised the bottle before splashing some onto the ground below. "I'll miss you, man."

Her gaze fell to the empty spot beside her. Mikey sat there. Lin sat there. Her throat was suddenly tight. She wasn't ready to be alone.

TWENTY-EIGHT

Rocks skittered under Nel's boots. She had thought a thousand times about this moment for the past month. She still did not believe it had come. She tucked the box to her chest. Mikey didn't deserve to be shoved into a backpack pouch with expired sunscreen and a sandwich from last season. The hill had not changed, but her knees were weak by the time she tottered into the cave's entrance. The turquoise water chattered through the rock face, and Nel laid Mikey on an outcropping while she shucked off her boots. Some things were meant to be done as soul-bared as possible, and boots were not part of that picture.

The box was warm in her hand, sunwarmed, but also body-warm and breath-warm. It seemed fitting that under the high noon light, that they both would seek shade in the ancient shelter.

Nel carefully undid the top, tapping the displaced grey dust from the lid before laying it aside. She sat carefully beside it, feet trailing in the water. "It's been a while since I talked to you. I don't think you can hear me, that you're up on some cloud listening, don't worry. But maybe you're in the fish here. Maybe you're in the water. Maybe you're somewhere up in the stars. Maybe you'll be part of what Lin needs for her family to find their way back."

She dipped two fingers into the water, then his ashes. The body was ephemeral, really. The fear-rooted embalming, pretending at life, was only more painful. *You can't grieve if they're still there. If you never accept they're gone.* Nel had never been a griever, but she had never lost someone as integral to her being, to the career she had built, as Mikey.

She trailed her fingers into the water again, letting ash disappear downstream. "Dammit, Mikey, I guess you'll get me to sing after all." She cleared her throat softly. "Amazing grace, how sweet the sound that saved a wretch like me." Her fingers brushed ashes, water, ashes, water. Her voice did not soar in the canyon, rather the sound stumbled against the stone as she let Mikey go, the whisper of ashes washed from her hands.

"And we've been there ten thousand years as bright shining as the sun." She botched half the lines, humming through the words she was uncertain of, and singing the chorus more than she figured was accurate. Finally, the box was all but empty, and her fingers were pruned with their continued swim. She trailed a finger around the inside of the box and pressed it to her lips. The ashes tasted like sand, but she smiled. "You may be a thousand things now, but you'll also be in my bones."

She rose with a sigh and began the trek back up the hill. The low slung sun painted the sky a soft almost-green at the edge of the blue of dusk. A battered car stood behind the jeep. Emilio leaned on one open door, his expression that of patience and understanding. He watched her clamber over the rail, gaze brushing red eyes and lighter shoulders. Still, he waited to speak until she raised her hand in greeting.

"This is a good place."

She nodded. "When we were first here, he said this is where he'd want his ashes, some of them, at least."

He hummed in acknowledgement. His eyes remained fixed on the sky for another minute before easing himself up onto the hood of his car. "We have a story about this place, you know."

"A Los Pobladores story, or a another kind?"

"I think they are the same."

She smiled faintly. "Perhaps you're right." She hoisted herself up beside him, leaning back on her elbows. "You gonna tell it, or just tease me?"

He grinned. "You are full of impatience, Bently. It's a good story, but not one for today." He gestured, patient and gentle, to the canyon. "My father said when our ancestors were new, this world was already old. Our people first began to search. When you find what you're searching for, you come find me and I'll tell you the story."

"But I'm always searching, remember?" She leaned her head back, staring at the first, dim stars. "I think searching, exploration, is a home of sorts. Looking for a greater sense of home. Besides, without exploring, without those questions that lead us there, we wouldn't have stories to tell, now would we?"

Emilio's eyes flicked to her and softened. "Perhaps we say the same thing, just in different words."

END

Check out this sneak peek at the next
Nel Bently Book:

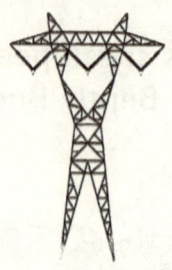

ONE

Nel's cell rattled in the cup holder in the center console, and she sighed. Probably Martos, making sure she wasn't going to bail on her meeting. She slid her thumb across the screen. "Yeah?"

"Hey, honey, how're you doing?"

"Oh, hey, Mom. All right."

"How was your flight? When'd you get in?"

Nel grinned at the barrage of questions. As much as they all joked that Nel was the clone of her father, the older she got, the more she realized that she was really a mixture of her parents. "I'm driving, so I can't really talk, but I got in Saturday night. Flight was fine. Had some turbulence and stuff, and a crying baby, but that was it." She could almost picture her flight-terrified mother's shudder.

"Glad I wasn't there. Where are you headed?"

"To the school. I have a meeting with the department. Martos wants me to bring up tenure, and I'm sure I'll hear a ton about the site and safety and responsibility."

"They don't actually think it was your fault, do they?" Rustling clothes and the sound of clinking dishes told Nel her mom was unloading the dishwasher.

"I don't know what they think, really, but I'm sure it's not pretty. The problem is the situation was dangerous, and I had kids down there. I'm kinda stressed about it all."

Her mom hummed in sympathy and the background noise stopped as she paused to focus on the conversation. "You call me afterward, all right? We can talk it out. And maybe you can come down for dinner this week?"

Nel smiled. Her mom was a good listener. "Yeah, I'll call. Not sure about dinner, things are really gearing up for the semester, and I'm supposed to take on a bunch of Mikey's stuff."

"I'll send Bill to play billiards with the fire department guys."

"How does Thursday sound?" Nel offered. She loved seeing her mom, and a meal she didn't have to cook herself was a rarity. It wasn't always worth dealing with her stepdad and his opinions.

Nel's mom snorted. "I thought so. Thursday's good for me. I'll let you know later if I can shoo him out that night. When is your meeting finished?"

"Noon. I'll call you then?"

"All right, sweetie. Good luck. Love you!"

"Love you, too." Nel tapped her phone and dropped it back into the cup holder. Her stomach wasn't as tight as before. The only person who settled her mind as much as Mikey was her mom. She spun the wheel and turned down University Ave. The broad street was separated by a row of flowering trees and abstract art installations. An undulating fountain stood under the broad arched entrance to the college. It was sputtering and green, as it usually was in the summer, but in two weeks she was sure it would sparkle. Nel slammed the brakes on as a group of boys stumbled into the road on their way across campus. "Get out of the fucking road, you idiots!"

One flipped her off, then saw her professor-parking pass and scooted after his friends.

"Yeah, that's right you little asshole." She turned into the parking lot and found a spot near the rear of the lot. She pressed her forehead against the rim of the steering wheel and drew a breath. There was nothing to worry about.

"What's the worst-case scenario?" Mikey always had a way to rationalize her out of a panic.

"They fire me."

"So what? You've got the creds. You can teach plenty of places. Maybe not as hip as USNE, but still something."

She steadied her thoughts before tugging her bag from the passenger seat and heading toward the sprawling multi-addition Social Studies building.

A tall woman emerged from the student union, black hair a sail in the wind and rain. Business casual looked that good on only one woman.

"Lin?" Nel broke into a jog, the movement awkward with her bag. "Lin!"

The woman disappeared into the science center. Nel pushed through the gleaming double doors a moment later. The wide halls were deserted. No footsteps clacked on the tiles. She slumped against the glass with a sigh. *I'm seeing things now.* Thunder muttered in the distance.

She glanced at her phone. Fifteen minutes—just enough time to collect herself and drop things at her desk. Every thought grew both heavy and frantic as Nel jogged across the quad to her building. Six months ago, the only goal left on her career list was attaining a tenured position. Working with a smaller university that focused more on published papers and teaching ability than seniority brought her goal that much closer. It hurt that she might not achieve it now, depending on the meeting. What hurt worse, though, was a large part of her no longer cared. It was the same part that howled into the void in her chest where Mikey used to be.

She strode through the History wing and into the breezeway between the original part of the building and the first addition. She tugged the package from her bag with a sigh. Reading the details of her permit revocation was depressing, but she should be up-to-date for the meeting.

Multiple seals and stamps decorated the heavy bubble-pack. None were of her local post office.

Dr. Annalise Bently
C/o Lin Nalawangsa
IDH Atlantic Headquarters,
4 Endeavour Ln
Oromocto, NB, E2V4T9

Nel whirled to peer at the science center across the way. *It was her. She can drop a package on my stoop but can't respond to a text?*

She tugged the tab, expecting a thick document. Instead, a cheap cell phone dropped into her hand. It was new, and off-brand, the kind box-stores sold minute cards for. Frowning, she flipped it open and held down the power button. The chime was tinny. It was fully charged and had prepaid minutes through the end of the month. A cartoon UFO decorated the background. *What the fuck?*

She thumbed to the message box. There was only one, from a contact titled "Mothership." She rolled her eyes and looked at the message:

> *Text 'Received' and your surname when this arrives.*

It was a joke, and a sick one at that, but she couldn't ignore her curiosity. She did as it asked, and trotted up the stairs to the lobby of the Anthropology wing.

"Dr. Annalise Bently?"

Nel glanced up. Two campus security officers blocked the doorway to her department. A suited white man stood a step in front, holding up his FBI badge. "Dr. Bently is fine," she replied, stopping several steps away. Fear flashed through her veins.

"Ma'am, I'm Special Agent Pheters. You oversaw the Los Cerros Esperando VII this past summer, correct?" A thick Maine accent pulled at his clipped words

"Yes, I did." Nerves screamed at her.

"The Chilean police found a body yesterday." He glanced at the few research assistants and aides milling around. "You need to come with us."

"I haven't been on site for over a month." The new phone buzzed in her hand. Her fingers tightened around it.

"The body has your DNA on it," Pheters explained. "We need to bring you in."

"For arrest?"

"Don't make a scene in front of your students." Condescension belied the kindness of the man's words.

Adrenaline exploded through her body. The wet grind of her trowel through flesh filled her mind. *Lin said there were no bodies. She said I'd be safe.* Her eyes flicked up to the agent before glancing at the phone. An incoming text opened on the screen.

RUN

And she did.

Explore the events leading up to
Travelers through Lin's eyes in:

Disciples

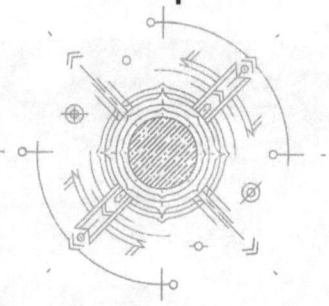

Cryosleep was a temporary death. The lights were dim, a twilight between waking and sleep. Lin blinked and rolled her shoulders, stretched her neck, curled her toes. Viscous stasis fluid drained silently, leaving goosebumps across her beige skin. Nausea shuddered through her. She ignored it. Instead she drifted in the peace of momentary amnesia. The hiss of heated air punctured the stillness. She flexed her fingers and tapped the smooth metal embedded in the flesh of her wrist. "Commence waking sequence in five...." She counted the seconds down silently.

"Good morning, Opsir Nalawangsa." The low voice was male, and just shy of truly human. The lights rose, gradual and faintly yellow.

"Good morning, Phil. Where are we?" She pushed out of her tank, rising in the zero G of her cryo tube. The lights were fully bright now.

"We're in orbit, 437 km from the surface of the planet Earth." There was a pause, and she almost thought the ship's voice held a smile. "Welcome home."

She snorted. "My genes may come from that ball of dirt, Phil, but I certainly don't." The air rolled over her skin, drying as it went. A click and pop echoed from beside the closed door of the cryo tube. She grabbed the vial from the ship's delivery system and held it up.

NALAWANGSA, LIN
IMMUNIZATION LEVEL 2
STABILIZERS
PROTEIN
CARBOHYDRATES
ELECTROLYTES
VITAMINS A, D, B, C
SALINE

She groaned. "What does a woman have to do to get proper grilled fish with her breakfast in bed?"

"When you cure cryo-sick I will personally deliver you a plate of fresh milkfish in bed upon waking."

She rolled her eyes and snapped the vial into the port in her arm. A moment passed then her nausea subsided. Aching in her head ebbed. "How was the trip?"

"Uneventful. You are wanted in Trajectory." Phil's tone often trod the line between a butler's deference and a captain's rebuke.

"Dar?"

"Yes. It appears Komodor Muda Nalawangsa has requested you personally. Shall I tell him you're on your way?" *Probably just to rub in his new rank of Komodor Muda and the fact he's now senior enough to just 'request' me.* "Thanks, Phil. I'll see you there." She unwrapped the plastic from her uniform and slid it on. After seven years of drifting naked in a vat of saline, the stiff electro-fiber felt cumbersome. She flexed her hand, aligning the contacts inside with the conduits tattooed on her skin. A hum. A rush of energy not-quite-her-own. *Paired.* The word wasn't spoken, not heard in the traditional sense, nor was it a thought. It least, not hers. *Increase temperature by 0.5 degrees C.*

Her goosebumps sank back into her skin. She slid the door open and slithered from her cryotube. The lights here were brighter, the snaking lines of green and blue illuminating the stark white of walls and the sharp silver of glass. Her finger brushed the pad in the wall, changing a panel from cycling photos to a mirror. She scraped her hair back and straightened her collar. It was always alarming how little her face changed during years of cryosleep.

"Opsir Nalawangsa—"

"Yeah, Phil, I know. On my way." She shoved through the next door into a corridor. The steep curve told her still-disoriented mind she was on the interior of the ship. A gentle press indicated they were just inside the gravitational field. *Planet-side is starboard.* She kicked off the floor and sailed along the corridor. Other than several bots and the usual techs, the hall was deserted. *Debriefing already started then.* It took days for the ship and crew to recover from a cryo-trip to open space. Longer when they arrived at a planet's orbit. She found the first drop-door to the exterior rings of the ship and pressed the symbol for Trajectory. The ground trembled with the rings' gentle turning. When the doors between the outer rings and a transport shaft were aligned the door slid open. Lin dropped, her grin broad. This was her favorite part. The slight artificial gravity brought by the rotation grew the farther from the core she got, so what started as a gentle drift accelerated into a true free fall.

WARNING: Falling from high places can result in damage or expiration. Engage mag-catch. She ignored the suit for another moment, enjoying the rushing air. Lights flickered past as she hurtled through dozens of levels. She clenched her teeth against biting her tongue. *Suit: Engage mag-catch.* Electromagnets in her suit kicked on with a hum and lurch. By the time she arrived at the door emblazoned with the symbol for Trajectory she was floating. A panel slid across the transport tube and she touched down. Gravity settled over her like a blanket. Even her organs felt heavy. Her palm on the door granted access to the waiting area. Another palm on the next door prompted a cheery robotic voice very unlike Phil's.

"Good morning! Please state your rank, full name, and purpose clearly into the speaker."

Lin leaned forward. "Opsir Muda Udara First Class Lin Nalawangsa, to see Komodor Muda Udara Dar Nalawangsa."

"Accepted, have a lovely day!"

Lin smiled, wondering if the security bot's voice grew irate when you weren't allowed through. The door slid open and she stepped through. Trajectory was as messy and chaotic as the rest of the ship was tidy. The bank of screens to the left showed their past trips, and those of other ships in the fleet. One blinked with a digital scan of Phil's face as he debriefed the crew and discussed issues with other ships' minds. The right was a whirlwind of orbit physics and gravitational maps. Her brother stood within the ring of navigation and communication computers that dominated the center of the room. He snarled something at the image of Phil's head on one of his screens. "I don't really care what the ISS has to say. Our orbit takes precedence. It's much harder for us to navigate then for them."

"Sir," Phil offered, "I think they feel differently. They're expecting a shipment and new crew. Their flightpath has been planned for months, and the weather won't hold forever—"

"I'll show them fucking weather..." His mutter almost drowned in a chorus of beeps that rose from Navigation. "Then put me on the comm with NASA."

"Paging NASA."

Lin saw her opening and stepped up to the raised floor of the Captain's Ring. "You wanted to see me, Dar?"

Dar frowned, but did not look up. He could have been her twin: black, smooth hair, warm beige skin, and deep oval eyes. Their features and parents, however, were the only things they shared.

"I need you to go planet-side."

Lin's stomach lurched. The tingle crawling up her arms had nothing to do with electromagnets or her suit maintaining temperature. "Excuse me?"

Read the rest for free at vsholmes.com/disciples

CHAD

The character of Chad is born from a man of the same given name—Chad Di Gregorio. I met Chad in Greece during my first dig. While I only knew him for a short time I learned quickly that he was a man of kindness, dedication, and intelligence. He was a fantastic archaeologist who impacted many lives. He left this world far too soon, and it is in his honor I wrote Nel's colleague.

Chad was a wonderful human, of whom I can only hope to portray a fraction.

GLOSSARY

Alluvial sands - Soil deposited by running water, such as streams, rivers, and flood waters. (Archaeological Institute of America, 2015)

ALMA - Atacama Large Millimeter/submillimeter Array is the largest astronomical project in existence. It is a single telescope of revolutionary design located on the Chajnantor plateau of northern Chile. (Atacama Large Millimeter/submillimeter Array, 2015)

Artifact - A portable object manufactured, modified, or used by humans. (Archaeological Institute of America, 2015)

Backdirt - The excavated, discarded material (sediment, dirt) from a site that has generally been sifted for artifacts and is presumed to be of no further archaeological significance. This material may later be used to refill test pits, an action referred to as "back filling." (Archaeological Institute of America, 2015)

Beringia - land bridge between Asia and North America exposed by low sea levels during the last Ice Age 110,000 to 12,000 years ago. It is now under the Bering Strait. (National Geographic Genographic Project. 2015)

Biface - Stone tools that have been worked on both sides or faces, meaning that flakes have been intentionally (not naturally) chipped off from both sides of the stone. (Archaeological Institute of America, 2015)

Chert - Chert and flint were the main sources of tools and weapons for Stone Age peoples. Because of the uniformly fine grain, brittleness, and conchoidal fracture of flint and chert it was relatively straightforward to flake off chips to shape them, leaving razor edges. (Bonewitz et. al., 2005)

Chipping debris - see *debitage*

Clovis - Clovis is the name archaeologists have given to the earliest well-established human culture in the North American continent. Clovis were the first big game hunters of the Paleoindian tradition, although they were probably not the first people in the American continents. Clovis archaeological sites are dated between 12,500 and 12,900 calendar years before the present and they are found pretty much throughout North America. (About Education. 2015)

Contract Archaeology - archaeological research, survey and excavation undertaken under contracts with government agencies, private organizations or individual landowners. (Central Archaeological Group Inc. 2016)

CRM - Cultural Resource Management. Profession that focuses on the management and preservation of cultural resources, such as archaeological sites or artifacts, protecting them for future generations. (Archaeological Institute of America, 2015)

Debitage - Small pieces of stone debris that break off during the manufacturing of stone tools. These are usually considered waste and are a by-product of production. (Archaeological Institute of America, 2015)

Diagnostics - artifacts that are indicative of a specific culture or time period.

Feature - A structure or physical element, such as a living surface, hearth, or pit altered or made by humans or human habitation. Features cannot be transported from a site, unlike an artifact. (Archaeological Institute of America, 2015)

Fishtail point - A projectile point with a leaf-like blade and a narrow stem that flares out at the very base, giving it the appearance of a fish's tail. Fishtail points are associated with the earliest hunter-gatherers in South America.

Flake - A piece of stone removed from a core for use as a tool or as debitage. (Archaeological Institute of America, 2015)

Fluted point - spear or dart points that have been bifacially flaked, characterized by a central flute or channel flake and a concave base enclosed by small, thin ears. (Museum of Anthropology. 2015)

GIS - Geographic Information System is a computer system for capturing, storing, checking, and displayingdata related to positions on Earth's surface. GIS can show many different kinds of data on one map. This enables people to more easily see, analyze, and understand patterns and relationships. (National Geographic Education. 2016)

Hematite - a dense, hard iron oxide often red in color. Sometimes used to make ceremonial red ocher. Due to a high iron content of 70% it can be magnetized. (Bonewitz et. al., 2005)

Knapping - A technique for making stone tools and weapons by striking flakes from a core with a hard (stone) or soft (antler) percussion instrument. Individual flakes or cores can be further modified to create tools. Also called flintknapping. (Archaeological Institute of America, 2015)

Lithics - artifacts made from stone. (Archaeological Institute of America, 2015)

Mapuche - The Mapuche people are the original inhabitants of a vast territory in what is now Chile and Argentina. In Chile the Mapuche live mainly in the provinces of Bio-Bio, Arauco, Malleco, Cautin, Valdivia,

Osorno, Llanquihue and Chiloe. (Intercontinental Cry, 2015)

Molcajete - traditional mortar and pestle from Latin American countries. Has three, often conical legs and a broad, shallow bowl and is typically made of ground stone.

Monte Verde - Archaeological site located in Acclaimed in 1997 as the earliest known site in the Americas and the first undoubted pre-Clovis site (Archaeology Archive. 2015)

Munsell - The Munsell Soil Color Book is filled with colored tiles carefully organized into families and rows/columns of reds and yellows as well as a few other, rarer soil colors. It allows universal identification of soil colors.

Osteology - The study of the structure and function of bones. (Archaeological Institute of America, 2015)

Paleolithic - The early stage of the Stone Age, beginning about 750,000 years ago. During this time humans relied on stone technology to sustain their scavenging, hunting and gathering lifestyle. (Archaeological Institute of America, 2015)

Perimortem - at or near the time of death; in perimortem injuries, bone damage occurring at or near the time of death, without any evidence of healing. (Smithsonian National Museum of Natural History. 2015)

Phase II - archaeological testing of a site previously identified through Phase I survey. Phase II survey determines horizontal and vertical boundaries of a site as well as significance.

Prehistoric - The period of human history preceding written records. (Archaeological Institute of America, 2015)

Projectile point - stone point affixed to the shaft of an arrow, dart, or spear.

Protein residue analysis - Protein residue analysis is used to identify the presence of prehistoric, historic, or even modern proteins, both animal and plant. (PaleoResearch Institute. 2010)

Radiocarbon dating - An absolute dating technique used to determine the age of organic materials less than 50,000 years old. Age is determined by examining the loss of the unstable carbon-14 isotope, which is absorbed by all living organisms during their lifespan. Dates generated by radiocarbon dating have to be calibrated using dates derived from other absolute dating methods, such as dendrochronology and ice cores. (Archaeological Institute of America, 2015)

Scoria - Scoria is a dark-colored igneous rock with abundant round bubble-like cavities known as vesicles. It ranges in color from black or dark gray to deep reddish brown. It is often carved into molcajete, ceremonial artifacts and, most famously, the heads of Easter Island. (Geoscience News and Information: Geology.com. 2015)

Shovel Test Pit - An excavation unit used in the initial investigation of a site or area, before large-scale excavation begins, that allows the archaeologist to "preview" what lies under the ground. (Archaeological Institute of America, 2015)

Silicate - silicates contain silicon and make up about 25 percent of all known minerals, 40 percent all the most common ones. (Bonewitz et. al., 2005)

Spectroscopy - Spectroscopy pertains to the dispersion of an object's light into its component colors (i.e. energies). By performing this dissection and analysis of an object's light, astronomers can infer the physical properties of that object (such as temperature, mass, luminosity and composition). (University of Arizona. 2015)

Strata - The layers (strata) of sediments, soils, and material culture at an archaeological site. (Archaeological Institute of America, 2015) (See Fig. 3)

Stratigraphy - The study of the strata at an archaeological site (also used in geology for the study of geological layers). (Archaeological Institute of America, 2015)

Total station - An optical surveyor's instrument that combines a transit and an electronic distance measuring device. A total station calculates angles and distances for surveyed objects. This information can be used to create topographic maps. (Archaeological Institute of America, 2015)

Unit - An excavated area measuring 1m or 2m square. Multiple units will make up a larger grid.

YBP - Years Before Present

Sources

About Education. 2015. "The (pre) History of the Clovis - Early Hunting Groups of the Americas." Retrieved July 23, 2015 (http://archaeology.about.com/od/clovispreclovis/qt/clovis_people.htm)

Archaeological Institute of America. 2015 "Introduction to Archaeology: Glossary." Retrieved Dec. 3, 2015 (https://www.archaeological.org/education/glossary)

Archaeology Archive. 2015 "Online Features: Monte Verde Under Fire." Retrieved June, 4, 2015 (http://archive.archaeology.org/online/features/clovis/)

Atacama Large Millimeter/submillimeter Array. 2015. "About ALMA." Retrieved Aug. 9 2015 (http://www.almaobservatory.org/en/about-alma)

Bonewitz, Carruthers, and Efthim. 2005. *Rock and Gem.* New York, NY: Dorling Kindersley Limited

Casanova, Salazar, Seguel, and Luzio. 2013. *The Soils of Chile.* New York, NY: Springer.

Central Archaeological Group Inc. 2016 "What is Contract Archaeology?" Retrieved Jan 4 2016 (http://www.centralarchaeology.ca/what-is-contract-archaeology)

Geoscience News and Information: Geology.com. 2015 "What is Scoria." Retrieved Dec. 5 2015 (http://geology.com/rocks/scoria.shtml)

Intercontinental Cry 2015 "Indiginous Peoples Archive, Latest Articles: Mapuche." Retrieved January, 1, 2016 (https://intercontinentalcry.org/indigenous-peoples/mapuche/)

Museum of Anthropology. 2015 "Paleoindian Archaeology: Clovis Stone Tools." Retrieved Dec. 3 2015 (https://anthromuseum.missouri.edu/minigalleries/clovistools/intro.shtml)

National Geographic Education. 2016 "Geographic Information System." Retrieved Jan 3, 2016. (http://education.nationalgeographic.org/encyclopedia/geographic-information-system-gis/)

National Geographic Genographic Project. 2015. "Bridge to the New World." Retrieved Sept. 24 2015 (https://genographic.nationalgeographic.com/land-bridge/)

PaleoResearch Institute. 2010. "Protein Residue." Retrieved Nov. 14 2015 (http://www.paleoresearch.com/services/pra.html)

Smithsonian National Museum of Natural History. 2015. "Definition: Perimortem." Retrieved Dec. 3 2015 (http://anthropology.si.edu/writteninbone/comic/activity/pdf/Perimortem.pdf)

University of Arizona. 2015. "What is Spectroscopy?" Retrieved Dec 3 2015 (http://loke.as.arizona.edu/~ckulesa/camp/spectroscopy_intro.html)

Whittaker, John C. *Flintknapping: Making and Understanding Stone Tools.* 1994. Austin, TX: University of Texas Press.

ACKNOWLEDGEMENTS

Thank you to Dr. Tom Strasser of Providence College in Rhode Island, who led my first dig on Crete. Without you, I never would have known how amazing archaeology is.

Thank you to Dr. James Stemp of Keene State College in New Hampshire. Your guidance, your incredible knowledge and passion for other peoples—particularly the Maya of Belize—changed my path forever.

Thanks to you Dr. Richard Boisvert, State Archaeologist of New Hampshire. Your field schools gave me the valuable tools for my career and your continued humor and drive is truly inspiring.

Lastly, but certainly not least, thank you to the phenomenal people I work with every day protecting the cultural resources of our world. Your stories, antics, and kindness have built this series. Perhaps you will see your own tales woven into the fabric.

ABOUT THE AUTHOR

V. S. Holmes is an international bestselling author. They created the BLOOD OF TITANS series and the NEL BENTLY BOOKS. *Smoke and Rain*, the award-winning first book in their fantasy quartet, became an international bestseller in 2018. *Travelers* is also included in the Peregrine Moon Lander mission as part of the Writers on the Moon Time Capsule. In addition, they write game content for Stone Blade Entertainment.

As a disabled and **non-binary** human, they work as an advocate and educator for representation in SFF worlds. When not writing, they work as a contract archaeologist throughout the northeastern U.S. They live with their spouse, a fellow archaeologist, their dog Rory, and own too many books.

www.vsholmes.com

www.ingramcontent.com/pod-product-compliance
Lightning Source LLC
Chambersburg PA
CBHW031238120726
47905CB00002B/648